QUOTE FOR A KILLER

by

J.D. MALLINSON

Waxwing Books, New Hampshire

Copyright 2013 by J.D. Mallinson

ISBN-13:978-1492830603

Inspector Mason novels:

Danube Stations
The File on John Ormond
The Italy Conspiracy
The Swiss Connection

CHAPTER ONE

When Detective Inspector George Mason reached Scotland Yard on Monday morning, he found Chief Inspector Bill Harrington waiting impatiently for him. From the concerned look on the other's face, he sensed that a new assignment was in the offing.

"Step into my office," Harrington urged, "and take a seat. There's something I want you to look into without delay."

Mason followed him in and sat facing him across an unusually tidy walnut desk, wondering whether the Chief Inspector was not about to slide open the bottom drawer and pour himself a tot of his favorite malt whiskey. Harrington's right hand did in fact hover momentarily in that area, but now with both hands clasped and his lips tightly pursed, he gave his colleague a long, searching look. George Mason waited patiently, not knowing quite what to expect.

"Your recent cases," the Chief Inspector objectively remarked, "have taken you practically the length and breadth of Europe. Zurich, Vienna,

Budapest, you name it. You're becoming quite a cosmopolitan."

George Mason returned a diffident smile. It was all in a day's work to him, and if he'd had the opportunity to travel professionally, so much the better. It helped improve his knowledge of languages, and of human nature.

"I thought you'd appreciate something closer to home, by way of a change."

"Has something new come in?"

"An incident in the City," Harrington explained. "The manager of National Indemnity was shot point-blank shortly after arriving at his office this morning. An ambulance was called and he was transferred to East London Hospital."

"Any news of his condition?" Mason asked, with concern.

"Not so far. At least, nothing further has come through to this office. You'll find out more when you reach the premises."

"Located at...?"

"Ropemaker Lane. My secretary has drawn up directions. You should take the District Line tube to Monument, proceed along Threadneedle Street past the Bank of England and you'll be almost there."

"I shall get onto it straight away," Mason said, rising from his chair and moving towards the door.

"Oh, and by the way," Harrington called after him, "for support, you can avail yourself of the services of Detective Sergeant Alison Aubrey. She's being transferred as of tomorrow morning to Scotland Yard, from the Sussex Constabulary. The Commissioner was impressed with the way she handled herself on your Zurich assignment together and thought her career would benefit from a spell at HQ."

"Glad to hear it," Mason replied, with a smile.

Making a mental note to contact Alison early tomorrow morning, George Mason left the office without taking time to check his mail, quit the building and crossed the busy street, before disappearing down the steps at the entrance of Westminster Underground to catch the eastbound tube. In under half an hour he re-surfaced at Monument, taking the opportunity to admire the impressive structure built there by Sir Christopher Wren, architect of St. Paul's Cathedral, to commemorate the Great Fire of London. Pausing briefly to admire the stamina of the tourists mounting its three hundred steps, he continued past the Old Lady of Threadneedle Street, as the Bank of England was fondly called, to the premises of National Indemnity. Announcing himself at Reception, he was shown at once into the private office of the Assistant Manager, John Jeffries.

"Any news?" he immediately enquired.

Jeffries shook his head regretfully and seemed on the verge of tears.

"We received a phone call a short while ago," he explained. "Mr. Fields did not survive the attack. He died shortly after reaching the hospital."

"That is terrible news," Mason said. "My deepest sympathies."

"Thank you," Jeffries replied, with feeling. "My staff are in terrible shock over this. We have closed the retail counter for the rest of today, and the police have cordoned off the front entrance to the building."

"So I observed on my way in," the detective said. "Now what information can you give me about the incident that occurred this morning?"

The Assistant Manager cleared his throat and said:

"Very little, I am afraid. When Mr. Fields' secretary took him his morning coffee soon after we opened the front door, she found him slumped over his desk. I heard her scream, rushed into the adjoining office, realized immediately that he had been shot and dialed the emergency services. I then had at least the presence of mind to check the closed-circuit television. It showed a smartly-dressed individual enter the premises, cross the foyer and mount the stairs by the Reception desk. The receptionist was not at her post; apparently, she had just slipped into the restroom."

"And you have no idea who this intruder might be?"

"None whatsoever. On the recording, he looks for all the world like a typical bank client, but I do not recall any dealings with him. Yet he obviously knew his way round the building."

Having said that, he glanced with almost child-like optimism, tinged with angst, at his Scotland Yard visitor.

"What was the exact nature of your business?" Mason calmly enquired. "From your name, National Indemnity, I should have thought you were an insurance company rather than a bank."

John Jeffries for the first time that morning allowed himself the beginnings of a smile, a faint smile of appreciation at the detective's acumen.

"And you would have been quite correct," he said. "We did start out in insurance, but our directors extended our operations into the banking business to take advantage of the construction boom. There seemed to be a deal of money to be made, until..."

"...it all went south?" Mason quipped.

"Precisely," the other agreed. "I personally, as Assistant Manager, handle the insurance side of the business, which has remained largely profitable. For that reason alone, we have remained afloat as a financial institution, even after writing off hundreds of millions in bad loans."

George Mason said nothing for a while, weighing the other's words. A female staff member brought in fresh coffee, of which the Assistant Manager stood in obvious need. After it was served, he said:

"Do you think this attack on Mr. Fields might have had some connection with the nature of your business?"

Jeffries slowly sipped his coffee and said, deliberatively:

"That cannot be ruled out, Inspector. Several high-profile bankers in recent months have been subjected to personal assault in one form or another – on their homes, cars, yachts, for example. But never anything as extreme as this."

"It obviously wasn't in the nature of a robbery," the detective ruefully remarked. "Sounds more like a personal vendetta. Expand a little on the nature of your banking business."

"We began with a limited retail presence on the high street," Jeffries explained. "But in the push for higher profits, we began to specialize in loans to the construction industry."

"Apartment houses, office blocks, that sort of thing?" the detective asked.

Jeffries nodded in agreement.

"Add to that shopping malls and leisure complexes," he explained, "and our loan book increased rapidly over the last few years, to the extent that we became highly leveraged ourselves."

"What exactly do you mean by 'leveraged'?" a puzzled George Mason enquired.

"We borrowed heavily in the capital markets in order to finance our loans. When the market turned sour during the subprime crisis, we became overstretched and had to call in many of our loans. Or write them off."

"So you would have quite a number of disgruntled clients on your books? People who went to the wall because they couldn't repay the loans you made to them?"

John Jeffries drained his cup, replaced it carefully on the wooden tray and regarded his visitor with increasing respect. The Scotland Yard man, to his mind, possessed a better grasp of commercial affairs than he would have anticipated in a policeman.

"You can say that again, Inspector," he asserted. "Many are the ugly scenes that took place in this very office in recent months."

"Does anyone, to your mind, stand out particularly in that scenario?"

"We did quite a lot of business with Irish builders. Ireland, as you are probably aware, was among the countries hardest hit by the down-turn, with consequent heavy losses and unemployment, particularly in the construction industry."

"You were riding the back of the Celtic Tiger, in a manner of speaking?" his visitor asked.

The Assistant Manager allowed himself another thin smile at his visitor's perceptive and ironic remark.

"Conrad Fields came originally from Dublin," he explained. "He retained both family and business contacts there and, naturally, wanted to play a part in his home country's remarkable economic revival. We rather over-extended ourselves in that area, I'm afraid."

"A number of your Irish clients started to experience difficulties?"

"Exactly."

"Does anyone in particular come to mind?"

"I'll draw up a list of individuals who proved particularly truculent and fax it to you," Jeffries offered, "if you consider that is sufficient motive for murder. You may wish to start with Seamus Scully, who recently filed for bankruptcy. He practically raised the roof in this building one day last month when we informed him we were calling in his loan."

"Where would I find this gentleman?" George Mason asked, noting the name while suspecting that a trip across the Irish Sea was in prospect.

"He's staying at the White Hart Hotel in Cheapside," the other replied, "while his bankruptcy plea is moving through the courts."

The detective gave a scarcely audible sigh of relief at that and rose from his chair. On reaching the door, he said:

"I'll arrange for a police artist to come and look at your CCTV recording. He should be able to draw up a fairly accurate Identi-kit picture of the intruder."

"And I'll put that fax through as soon as possible," Jeffries promised, rising to see his visitor out. "Oh, and by the way, I found this slip of paper while going over documents on the manager's desk after he was taken to hospital."

He passed a typed note to Mason, who perused it at once, his brows knit in puzzlement.

"I can make neither head nor tail of it," the bank official said. "Perhaps it will mean something to you?"

The detective read it aloud:

"Money is the string Destiny uses to control its puppets."

"A literary quotation of some sort?" John Jeffries asked.

George Mason slowly nodded in agreement.

"Our killer is evidently something of a practical joker," he replied. "He also seems to have a philosophical bent and may well be a bit too clever for his own good. We shall see. I'll send our artist round as soon as I can arrange it, and I shall keep in touch."

With that, he slipped the note into his jacket pocket, left the premises of National Indemnity and retraced his steps to Monument tube station, where he took the District Line to Stepping Green to tie up some loose ends from one of his recent cases, the better to devote all his attention to this disturbing new development.

*

Detective Sergeant Alison Aubrey was in a buoyant mood as the early-morning train from Worthing, her home town, to London's Victoria Station sped through the Sussex Downs. It had just called at Haywards Heath, its last stop on the commuter line, and would reach London in less than an hour. She passed the time alternately dipping into Vogue magazine and glancing at the fleeting scenery through the carriage window. A strong coffee from the refreshment trolley helped calm her nerves as she thought of the new challenges that lay ahead. A step up to Scotland Yard so early in her career was a good omen, one that very few female officers from provincial police forces had made, and she had a shrewd idea in the back of her mind that George Mason might have had something to do with it. She knew he had given a good account of her abilities on his most recent European assignment, and that C.I.D. headquarters was looking to add more women for the gender balance. But she had never imagined that the choice would fall on her. Domestic arrangements fitted in, too. Following her first working day in London, she would take the tube to Maida Vale, where her married sister had a spare room, now that her eldest son was at college, in the Georgian Terrace home she shared with her surveyor husband, Cedric.

Alighting eventually at Victoria, she placed her suitcases in a left-luggage locker to retrieve later and walked smartly up the busy thoroughfare towards Scotland Yard, in order to present herself punctually at 9.00 a.m. Inspector George Mason was waiting to greet her.

"Good to see you again, Alison," he enthused, grasping her hand firmly. "Had a good trip up from Worthing?"

"Apart from the early start," she replied, agreeably surprised by the warmth of his greeting. "Had to rise at five-thirty to make the early train."

"Your first day in the big league," he remarked. "And guess what?"

Alison Aubrey regarded him cautiously, unsure quite what to expect.

"Your first assignment will be to assist me on a brand new case that's just come in."

The young policewoman smiled inwardly. She felt content at hearing that, and if she had harbored expectations during her journey of being given her own case to work on from Scotland Yard, she brushed that notion aside. One step at a time, she considered, and who better than the avuncular George Mason to ease her into her new role?

"What case would that be?" she enquired, assuming a professional air.

"A bank manager was shot dead in the City yesterday morning. Step into my office for a moment and I'll show you what we've got so far."

Seated facing each other across the cluttered desk, Mason showed her the likeness of the bank intruder which the police artist had completed the previous afternoon. Alison examined it closely.

"What's your reaction?" her colleague asked.

"Hard to say," she replied, "since it only shows him in three-quarter profile."

"A relatively young man, would you say?"

"Possibly, from the firmness of his features. He also seems quite bald, or close to it. Caucasian would be my guess."

"Which could include a Celt?" Mason remarked.

"Why do you say that?"

"Just a passing thought," he replied.

"Is this all we have to go on?" Alison then asked, in some surprise.

George Mason withdrew the slip of paper found on Conrad Fields' desk and passed it to her. The detective sergeant looked at it with puckered brow and read aloud:

"Money is the string Destiny uses to control its puppets."

"What do you make of that?" Mason challenged.

"I take it to mean that financial concerns of one kind or another are the dominant factor in people's lives. It could apply to rich or poor, the former being obsessed with increasing or preserving their wealth; the latter generally in dire need of money."

"Excellent, Alison. An astute reading," he said, with a growing impression that the young officer facing him was going to be an asset in solving this crime. "And where do you suppose this gem of wisdom originates?"

Alison Aubrey shrugged helplessly and said:

"I haven't the least idea. It sounds like something from Ecclesiastes or Proverbs, except that the Bible doesn't use words like Destiny. Providence would be more likely."

"This will be your first task," he then said, "to find the source of that quote."

"Where do you suppose I start?" she asked, a bit taken aback.

"Any good library," he replied. "It might take you a little while, but there's no hurry. I've got lots of spadework to do myself. Get started on it right away and report back to me later."

Alison Aubrey felt a sense of relief at being able to get down to work so soon; it took her mind off other matters and delayed her first encounter with the formidable Bill Harrington, the department chief who was at this moment in conference with the Commissioner. She rose from her place, quickly left the building and made her way through heavy traffic to Westminster Public Library, to see if she could trace the source of the beguiling quotation, with no clear idea of where she should begin. The reference librarian would be her first recourse. George Mason, for his part, took a few minutes to sort through his accumulated correspondence and, since there was nothing urgent, left soon after his junior colleague and took the tube to the City, where he had arranged an interview with Seamus Scully at the White Hart Hotel in Cheapside.

CHAPTER TWO

Working from the list of National Indemnity's Irish clients that John Jeffries had faxed him, George Mason had obtained from the Eire police the names of those individuals who had booked flights to London on and around March 17, in connection with the St. Patrick's Day celebration at the Barbican Theatre. It would have provided a perfect opportunity for a disaffected bank client to arrange the murder of Conrad Fields and return quietly to the Irish Republic. At the top of this list was the name of Seamus Scully, the person who had recently caused an ugly scene in the bank manager's office. Mason, however, had swiftly eliminated him from his enquiries. Calling on him by arrangement in Cheapside, he learned that Scully had been one of the key organizers of Celtic Mist, a festival of Gaelic poetry, song and dance. He had been at the Barbican since eight o'clock that fateful morning. The detective had shared the list of the dozen or so names furnished by the Eire police with Detective Sergeant Aubrey; they had both spent the better part of the past week checking the whereabouts and movements of those persons on that day.

"So you have drawn a complete blank?" he said resignedly, when they finally met in his office to compare notes.

"Afraid so," Alison confessed. "Every one of the names you gave me has a perfectly sound alibi. Several of them, in fact, did not leave Eire until later that day. They took the afternoon flight from Dublin to Gatwick."

"Budget travel," Mason quipped. "A sign of the times."

"The two individuals who were already here in London that morning were staying at West End hotels, a fair distance from the City. Hotel staff confirmed that they did not check out until after breakfast."

"I didn't have any luck either," George Mason admitted. "Yet I have a pretty strong hunch that Conrad Fields' death was related to the bank's loan book."

"Did you check with his wife," Alison asked, "to see if there were marital problems?"

"You mean, was she having an affair and persuaded her lover to remove her husband from the scene?"

"It does happen, George," his young assistant tentatively suggested.

"Anne Fields was quite distraught at the death of her husband. They were a very close couple, by all accounts. Together for over twenty years."

"Children?"

"A son at Imperial College, studying engineering."

"So we can rule out the jealous lover theory?"

"It would seem so," Mason said. "In any case, this incident cries out to be linked to finance in one way or another. The ailing construction industry seemed the likeliest lead, but failing that we shall have to widen our remit. That quotation I left you with, Alison. Any luck with it?"

The detective sergeant returned a smile of satisfaction.

"It took me over an hour the other morning to unearth it," she announced. "But unearth it I did."

"Out with it," Mason urged. "Don't keep me on tenterhooks."

"It's from Somerset Maugham," she informed him.

"Author of The Razor's Edge?" her impressed colleague enquired.

The young officer nodded.

"I was directed by the Reference librarian at Westminster to a Dictionary of Quotations," she continued. "Fortunately for me, the contents were arranged as to subject."

"So you looked up money and finance?"

"It was a very long section. It seems almost everybody who was anybody has had something to say on the subject."

George Mason pondered the information for a few moments.

"But why would a killer drop a quotation like that?' he asked, eventually.

"It suggests someone with a distinct literary bent," Alison said.

"That could be a very useful tid-bit in the days ahead," her colleague considered. "Seems like we're dealing with some kind of joker."

"So what will be our next move, after the Irish connection?"

"I haven't entirely given up on that angle," Mason replied. "But I did take the opportunity, while in the City the other day, of calling back on John Jeffries, the Assistant Manager of the bank. He informed me that Conrad Fields made several trips to Jersey in recent months. Jeffries does not know the reason for the visits and, in any case, the banking side of National Indemnity was kept strictly separate from the insurance business, which was Jeffries' bailiwick. He did give me the impression, though, that the Jersey visits were very hush-hush."

"How do you propose to follow that up?" Alison asked.

"I've asked Jeffries, who is now acting manager, to look into Fields' records and see if he can come up with the purpose of those visits, and whether transfers of funds were involved. It may be that we shall be taking a trip to the Channel Islands ourselves."

"I should love that," Alison said. "I've always wanted to visit St. Helier."

"You may well get the opportunity," George Mason conceded.

At that point, Chief Inspector Bill Harrington entered the office. From the grim look on his face, his two subordinates feared the worst. The senior officer sat down heavily in a spare chair and, with a glance towards the young detective sergeant, said:

"And how is our new recruit settling in?"

Alison flushed slightly at being the focus of attention from two men, who now regarded her with almost paternal interest.

"She's doing just fine," Mason said, speaking for her. "She's already turned up something that could be quite useful in this case."

"In what direction are your enquiries heading?" Harrington wanted to know.

"The construction industry," Mason replied. "National Indemnity specialized in loans to property developers, mainly in the Irish Republic."

"I'm afraid you may have to look a bit farther afield than Dublin," the Chief Inspector remarked. "In fact, you may be back on your European travels sooner than you expected."

His auditors riveted their gaze on him at that remark.

"You mean," George Mason began, "that there are wider ramifications?"

"The manager of Zuider Bank in Amsterdam was shot this morning, almost as soon as he entered his office. There may, of course, be no connection with the Fields incident in the City, but you'll have to get over there at once to co-ordinate enquiries with the Royal Dutch Police, in case there could be a link. Detective Sergeant Aubrey can hold the fort for you here, meanwhile, and handle any outstanding matters."

George Mason glanced quickly towards his young colleague, hoping she didn't feel side-lined. But she didn't seem in the least put out.

"It will give me time to settle down here in London and get my bearings," she remarked, as if reading his thoughts.

"So that's settled, Mason," Bill Harrington then said, rising to leave. "Your contact in Holland is Brigadier Klaas Brouwer, a rank equivalent to your own. There's a flight from Heathrow this afternoon at 4.12 p.m. Be on it."

*

George Mason arrived at Schiphol in the early evening, taking the rail link from the airport to Amsterdam Centraal. The train station, he discovered, opened onto a broad piazza lined with buildings that had changed little over time. This was the heart of the old trading city, its sidewalks lined with restaurants half-full of Amsterdamers and early visitors, cannabis tourists among them, he mused ironically. Hefting his heavy valise, he covered the short distance to the Herengracht, one of a series of broad canals that ringed the city, noting the elegance of former merchants' homes screened by newly-leafing trees, while regarding with a twinge of envy the colorful house-boats lining the quays. It was an unfulfilled ambition of his to live on a house-boat, perhaps somewhere along the Thames; it seemed such a self-contained, uncomplicated existence. Within an hour of his arrival, he had checked in at the Rijn Hotel, a modest establishment that Bill Harrington, who had prior knowledge of the city, had asked his secretary to book for him, having assured him of its high standards. George Mason sat down by his room window for a few minutes, to regain his breath, while watching the play of light over the canal. He eventually went down to the restaurant for dinner. Afterwards, to fill out the evening, he mingled with tourists exploring the elaborate system of waterways. A Venice of the North, without doubt, was his considered verdict, as he at length returned to his room to catch the ten o'clock news on television.

The next morning, immediately following breakfast, he took a cab to police headquarters. Brigadier Klaas Brouwer was expecting him. George Mason soon noted, to his relief, that he spoke fluent English.

"Chief Inspector Harrington mentioned that you've had a similar incident recently in the City of London," the Brigadier began, on completing the usual courtesies.

"It remains to be seen just how similar they are," his visitor remarked, not wishing to jump to premature conclusions.

"I'll drive you over to the premises of Zuider Bank straight away," the Brigadier said, "so that you can assess the situation for yourself."

With that, they climbed into a squad car and proceeded to an area somewhere beyond Centraal Station, where they pulled up before a rather drab commercial building set among geometric office blocks and Victorian warehouses well off the normal tourist beat. Brigadier Brouwer led the way in through the main entrance and up a flight of steps to the second floor, entering an office which had been cordoned off with yellow tape since the criminal intrusion of the previous day. The bank staff went about their normal business in adjacent areas, occasionally casting furtive glances in the direction of the two detectives.

"This is where the incident took place," the Dutch officer explained, "almost as soon as the bank opened its doors."

"The manager, Willem de Vries," Mason enquired, "did he survive the attack?"

"Yes...and no, in a manner of speaking," the other returned. "He retained consciousness on the way to the Royal Hospital and for a short time afterwards, but has since slipped into a coma. Prognosis is very uncertain."

"So you had some opportunity, at least, to speak with him?"

"He was able to give a very brief description of his assailant."

At this point, he drew out an Identi-kit picture, which George Mason immediately compared with the one he had brought with him from Scotland Yard. After a few moments, he said:

"They could well be the same individual. What's your opinion, Brigadier?"

The Dutch officer did his own careful comparison and nodded.

"Our likeness is fuller-face than yours, Inspector. Mr. de Vries thought he looked vaguely East European, which could mean anything – Pole, Russian, Balkan. You name it."

"Were any words exchanged?"

Klaas Brouwer shook his head.

"He quickly entered, fired one shot point-blank and hurried from the building."

"Mind if I take a look around?" Mason asked.

"Not at all, Inspector," the Dutch officer replied. "We've already done basic procedures."

George Mason crossed to the rear of the room, to the area near the office window and behind the manager's desk, scanning the furniture and carpet for anything that might have been overlooked, conscious that he was looking for one item in particular. At length, he examined the contents of the small waste bin, suddenly reached down and, with a gleam of triumph in his eye, held up a small piece of paper.

"What on earth have you got there?" the astonished Brigadier enquired.

"The very item I was hoping to find, to connect the two crimes."

The Dutchman returned a baffled look, awaiting further explanation.

"It's a quotation of some kind," Mason said, running it through his mind with a bemused smile. "On the subject of money."

"Aren't you going to share it?" Brouwer impatiently asked.

"Money is a kind of poetry."

"What on earth is that supposed to mean?"

"It is a clue," the Englishman explained, "in an odd sort of way. Or perhaps it could better be described as a taunt. This guy is playing games with us, Brigadier, which can only mean that he is supremely confident of avoiding detection. Something similar, a quotation from Somerset Maugham, was left at the London crime scene."

"You don't say so!" Klaas Brouwer exclaimed, in amazement.

At this point, the Deputy Manager, Pieter Fiske, returned from his visit to the Royal Hospital and immediately asked if he could be of help.

"Any improvement in Mr. de Vries' condition?" the Brigadier solicitously enquired.

Fiske shook his head, regretfully.

"But there is apparently some chance that he will recover," he explained, "since the bullet just missed his heart. His wife Leonie is with him now, keeping a bedside vigil."

"Tell me, Mr. Fiske," George Mason began, after expressing his concern, "what you know of the manager's business trips in recent weeks, particularly any trips abroad?"

The Deputy Manager glanced uncertainly at the Brigadier, as if wondering why this rather portly Englishman was asking the questions.

"It's all right, Mr. Fiske," Brouwer explained. "Inspector Mason and I are coordinating our enquiries."

Fiske cleared his throat and glanced from one to the other.

"Willem de Vries made several trips to London so far this year," he said. "I can give you exact dates from his diary, if you so wish."

"That would be most helpful," George Mason agreed. "Have you any knowledge of the purpose of these trips?"

"Routine banking business, I should say," Fiske rather cagily replied.

"You do not seem so sure," the Brigadier challenged. "I find that rather hard to understand."

The Deputy Manager shifted uneasily from one foot to the other.

"Mr. de Vries also made private visits to England," he said, with a suggestive smile. "I wouldn't wish to say anything that might cause him embarrassment."

"Were his business trips in connection with construction loans?" George Mason wanted to know, while taking Fiske's hint that his boss may have had romantic liaisons in England.

"Much of our business in recent months was in that area," Fiske conceded. "It seemed the place to earn substantial profits."

"Until the property market soured," Mason pointedly observed.

"That was the manager's province," the other asserted, rather defensively. "My responsibilities were mainly in routine administration and staff recruitment."

"I think you've told us what we need to know, for the time being," Brouwer then said, seeing that the man was anxious to get back to his normal duties. "Thank you for your help, Mr. Fiske."

He then turned to his visitor with a questioning look.

"What do I make of that, Brigadier?" Mason said, speaking for him. "Very little, frankly. You should get your forensic accountant over here quickly, to go through the books with a fine toothcomb and find out if monies have been transferred abroad. And for what purpose."

Klaas Brouwer immediately agreed on that course of action.

"Would you say that this is a second-tier bank?" Mason then asked. "One that is more likely to engage in the riskier type of business venture, in pursuit of quick profits?"

"Zuider Bank was implicated in money laundering about two years ago," the Brigadier replied. "But my impression is that they have since cleaned up their act. As far as riskier ventures go, our leading banks have been very heavily involved, much more so than the smaller fry, since they were able to borrow more. They call it leverage."

George Mason accepted that explanation without further comment. Twenty minutes later, they were back at Police Headquarters scanning computerized Wanted files, to see if they could match up the Identi-kit pictures with any known criminal.

"East European, de Vries seemed to think," Mason recollected.

"Interpol has just issued this file on former members of the Serbian army who have employed their talents in other directions since the conflict over Kosova," Brouwer explained.

"It hasn't reached Scotland Yard yet, to my knowledge," an intrigued George Mason remarked.

"It arrived here late yesterday," the other explained. "I spent most of last evening going over it. Some ex-servicemen became mercenaries in East Africa, for example. Others joined various private security corps in Iraq and Afghanistan; yet others got involved in dubious arms deals or human trafficking."

"It's a possible starting-point, at any rate," his visitor said. "But I would really be looking for someone with a more literary bent."

"How about this fellow, for example?" the undeterred Brigadier said, enlarging one of the file images.

Mason glanced from police sketch to computer, to compare the two. After several minutes, he said:

"I think we may well be onto something here. There is a distinct likeness around the eyes and the general shape of the face. The hair-style doesn't fit, but that could have been altered."

"Milovan Piric," the Dutch officer announced. "Sought in Hungary, in connection with an armed robbery in Debrecen two years ago, in which a security guard was killed. He's also suspected of complicity in the assassination of a Croatian government minister."

"In that case," Mason suggested, "you should put out a general alert through Interpol. I doubt you shall be able to apprehend him here in Holland. He's probably the type of criminal who moves around a lot. Meanwhile, let me know what your forensic accountant discovers regarding transfers of funds from Zuider Bank. I have to get back to London first thing tomorrow morning, and I'll take this cryptic quotation with me. My colleague, Detective Sergeant Aubrey is quite adept at tracing literary sources."

"Use the opportunity of seeing something of our beautiful city," Brouwer encouraged him, "while you are over here."

"I'll certainly do that," the other replied, aware that he had also been commissioned by Bill

Harrington to find a certain brand of cigar, and by his wife Adele to locate a Chanel scent.

Taking leave of the Brigadier, he made his way on foot back to the center of the old city to visit the shops. Tobacconists were on nearly every corner, and he soon found the half-coronas his chief required. Tracking down a rare perfume, however, was not so straightforward; it took him the remainder of the afternoon, in fitful spring sunshine, to find his purchase for Arlene at a boutique in a narrow street off the main shopping center. Having missed lunch, he was ready for his evening meal when he finally reached the small family restaurant a few doors down from the Rijn Hotel on the Herengracht, seeking a change from the hotel menu.

There was just a handful of locals dining at this early hour. The detective felt glad, as he studied the menu presented by an attractive blonde in traditional folk costume, that tourists were not yet much in evidence. It was still quite early in the season and most visitors would, in any case, most likely be at the tulip fields enjoying the riot of spring color. Following Bill Harrington's recommendation, he opted for the thick pea soup called snert to begin with; followed by a dish of mashed potatoes, mixed vegetables and smoked sausage that went by the name of hutspot. While awaiting service, he browsed through the copy of the London Times he had obtained at Centraal Station, to catch up on the news from England and the latest soccer scores. After a satisfying meal, he sat outside for a while on a canal-side bench to enjoy a small   cigar and observe the sporadic evening activity aboard the house-boats. He then took a cab to De Komedie Theatre, to occupy his final evening at a performance of Arthur Miller's All My Sons, presented by an American touring company. It was a toss-up between that and an evening of orchestral music at the Concertgebouw, under its guest conductor, SImon Rattle.

CHAPTER THREE

Around the same hour that George Mason was finishing his traditional Dutch fare, a slim, wiry individual with close-cropped thinning hair walked with a relaxed gait along the bracing Westerdijk seawall in Hoorn, a resort town on the North Sea thirty miles north of Amsterdam. He had holed up in this quiet watering place for the past few days, staying at the well-appointed Hotel Ibis while the initial alarm over the incident at Zuider Bank died down, and to await further instructions from the man he knew only as Jason. His path took him past the small, sheltered harbor, where he paused a few moments to watch the sturdy smacks heading out towards the fishing grounds, before making for the cosy seafront café on the edge of the Julianapark. By the time he reached it and ordered coffee with Dutch pancakes, the boats were already far out to sea.

At this early evening hour, the café was practically deserted. It was a favorite of vacationing families enjoying the amenities of the large park; they came here mainly for lunch, ice cream and light afternoon refreshments. Later on, teenagers below the legal drinking age would gather here to socialize and play popular music;

that would be the cue for his exit at around seven-thirty. This quiet, intermediate hour suited Milovan Piric. He could collect his thoughts without the racket of lively children or the swell from the juke-box. The food was plain but wholesome, the staff friendly. There was no way, he considered, that they could recognize him from the crude Identi-kit portrait on the front page of the leading Dutch broadsheet, De Telegraf, lying on the counter. He flattered himself that he was better-looking than the amateurish portrayal.

There was no reason either for the Royal Dutch Police to connect him with Zuider Bank. The Hungarian police would have been seeking perpetrators of an armed robbery two years ago at Debrecen, in the course of which his bungling accomplice had shot a security guard; but the case should by now have gone cold and relegated to the category of unsolved crimes. He had covered his tracks by signing on as a mercenary in East Africa, returning to Europe two years later via London. His successful negotiation of the British Immigration Service using his original passport, a deliberately calculated risk, persuaded him that the heat was off. As he dug into his appetizing shrimp pancake, he felt good reason to be satisfied with events over the past few years, since his army unit was disbanded following the war in Kosovo. Members of his family, Serbs living in Kosovo at the time, had been killed in the violence. He had then determined, partly out of anger, partly out of revenge at his perceived injustice of the conflict's outcome, to use his acquired military skills in the most profitable way possible.

Mercenary work had satisfied him for a time, and he had in fact quite enjoyed the rough-and-tumble of life in the African bush even if there never seemed to be any conclusive result from the armed struggle. But why, he had begun to wonder, should he be putting his life on the line to further other peoples' causes, just because the money was good? Security work in the Middle East was also highly remunerative, but it had similar drawbacks: a roadside bomb could result in serious injury or death.

On his return to Europe, he had discreetly advertized his services on the Internet and had received some curious replies, several of them from women who wanted to eliminate their husbands. The most promising, however, in that it involved ongoing prospects, was from an individual who referred to himself simply as Jason. They arranged to meet at The Devonshire Arms, an up-market pub in Chelsea with a clientele mainly of media and entertainment industry types. His contact, whom he estimated to be about fifty, with clean-cut features and short blond hair that put him somehow in mind of the film actor George Peppard, betrayed little of his own personal or professional life. He confined himself to outlining his unusual proposition and, having secured agreement on the fee, went on to give precise details of the operation. Milovan Piric had been a bit taken aback to learn that the first hit was to take place within days, in London's business district. He mentally ran through his few contacts in the London underworld, mainly ex-military like himself, to ensure he would have the required arsenal. They had then drained their pints of Flower's Bitter and parted company, as the comfortable tavern started to fill with animated regulars.

On returning to Hotel Ibis, he found a letter waiting for him. It was a note from Jason congratulating him on his two hits and advising him to lie low for a while, then make his way northwards into Scandinavia. His next set of instructions by mail would be waiting for him poste restante at The Old Post Office, Stockholm. The letter also included a bank draft for 25,000 euros, in part payment of the agreed fee. Milovan Piric flopped down on the narrow bed, his eye idly following the decorative plaster frieze along the top of the wall. The tasty meal, the brisk walk through the shoreline park on a fine spring evening, and now this encouraging communication from Jason, induced a mood of high contentment. He had long wanted to visit Scandinavia and now the opportunity was presenting itself. He would continue to relax in Hoorn, he decided, for the time being, then make his way back to Amsterdam. From Centraal Station, he would entrain to Hamburg, catch a ferry to Copenhagen and from there proceed to Malmo on the Swedish mainland. Now that he had adequate funds to hand, having transferred most of his mercenary income to a private bank in Switzerland, he could allow himself time to get properly acquainted with these attractive northern cities.

*

Towards the end of the week following his trip to Amsterdam, there were some positive developments for George Mason. Detective Sergeant Aubrey had finally traced the source of the curious quotation left at the scene of the Amsterdam crime. For some reason, it had proved more difficult to nail down than the Somerset Maugham quote, involving her in a visit to the Poetry Library at the South Bank Center.

"It's by Wallace Stevens," she announced, at the start of their morning conference.

"Who the Dickens might he be?" the perplexed detective enquired.

"He's a famous American poet, who died in 1955," Alison replied, with a knowledgeable air. "But not the easiest author to understand. Unlike, say, Walt Whitman or Robert Frost."

"Never heard of him."

"We encountered him briefly in literature seminars at school," the young woman went on. "Poems I fondly recall are The Emperor of Ice-Cream and The Man with the Blue Guitar. Our English teacher was quite keen on him."

"But what could it possibly mean to say that 'Money is a kind of poetry'?" Mason objected. "The converse, that poetry is a kind of money, is certainly not true. Have you ever heard of a rich poet?"

"It might mean," Alison ventured, "that there are all sorts of imaginative ways in which you can use money, the way a poet uses meter and images."

Mason took a short pause while digesting that gem of exegesis, before saying:

"Capital, Sergeant! I expect that's as good a reading as we are likely to get. You seem to have quite a knack at this type of thing."

"English was my favorite subject at school," Alison modestly replied, careful to avoid a sense of one-upmanship.

"So we have a gunman who quotes Somerset Maugham and Wallace Stevens," Mason said. "Brigadier Brouwer over in Amsterdam is convinced he's an ex-military man. It just doesn't add up."

"Puzzling, I agree. But isn't most detective work in the initial stages?"

"You're certainly right about that," Mason conceded. "Now what else do we have to go off?"

"Something just came through from Forensic Accounting," Alison said. "Our expert, Donald Dinwiddie…"

"A canny Scot, if ever there was one," her colleague interjected.

"...has traced large transfers of money from National Indemnity to a bank in St. Helier. Off the books, apparently."

"That's not too surprising," Mason remarked, "because Pieter Fiske telephoned from Zuider Bank about an hour ago that their people had identified similar transfers, again off the balance sheet, to the Aldgate branch of Kensington Bank here in London. Now, if we can determine that the transfers from Holland also ended up in Jersey, it strongly suggests some sort of collusion between Conrad Fields and Willem de Vries."

"An arrangement that was to cost them their lives?" Alison ruefully observed.

Mason nodded curtly, picked up the phone and rang through to Forensic Accounting.

"Dinwiddie," came the immediate response, in broad Scottish tones.

"Donald," the detective said, "can you elaborate on the transfers you identified from National Indemnity to Jersey? I need names."

The Scotsman cleared his throat noisily and consulted his notes.

"The receiving end was Sark Banking Corporation," he explained. "It's a small private firm that functions exclusively in the Channel Islands. The funds were directed there about two years ago, to an account in the name of Alderney Mortgages."

"A legitimate business concern, then?" the detective asked.

"On the face of it, yes," came the reply. "But if you wish to make certain, you will have to go down there yourself and make detailed inquiries. They're still very much alive. I already looked into that."

"That's most helpful of you, Donald. Much obliged."

He rang off and glanced pointedly towards Alison, who had overheard the brief conversation.

"Well," she asked, expectantly. "Are we...?"

"...going to Jersey, Sergeant? It's beginning to look that way, unless another incident occurs within the next few days and I have to leave at short notice to Paris, Brussels or some other European destination. First of all, I want you to go over to the Aldgate branch of Kensington Bank and interview the manager. We need to know if transfers were also made from there, starting about two years ago, to Sark Banking Corporation. If we can latch on to a money trail, we'll be making definite progress."

"I'll go over there straight away," she agreed. "Which tube should I take?"

"Circle Line, from Westminster," George Mason said. "It's only a few stops. You'll get the hang of the Underground system before long. It took me several weeks, I recall, after I was transferred from Yorkshire, before I became fully familiar with it."

*

Three days later, George Mason and Alison Aubrey took the mid-morning train to Southampton, where they boarded the ferry for the long trip down the English Channel to St. Helier, Jersey, experiencing a choppy voyage against strong south-westerlies rising in the Bay of Biscay. The younger officer, not the best of sailors, felt a sense of relief when they finally stepped ashore and headed towards The Crown Hotel on the main street. George Mason, on the other hand, had been in his element during the four-hour voyage. He enjoyed an ocean swell and spent most of the time strolling the decks, while Alison confined herself to reading magazines in the passenger lounge. No incidents similar to those in the City and in the Dutch capital had occurred meanwhile, allowing the detectives the leeway to pursue what appeared to be their best lead so far.

That the two bank incidents were linked, he had few doubts, since Alison had discovered on her visit to Aldgate that large sums of money had been transferred in stages from a branch of Kensington Bank to Sark Banking Corporation over the past two years. His original surmise, that Conrad Fields' death had some connection with construction loans, seemed increasingly plausible; except that it did not now appear, on the face of things, as if Irish builders were involved.

After settling in at their comfortable, family-run hotel and enjoying a dinner of fresh seafood with chilled Muscadet, they took a stroll along the promenade before returning, as it grew dark, to the hotel bar for a nightcap before retiring. Immediately after breakfast the following day, they set off to locate the premises of Alderney Mortgages in a narrow side-street in downtown St. Helier. At their entry the office manager, Celine Levasseur, rose to greet them.

"Scotland Yard?" she enquired in scarcely-veiled astonishment, as the two officers introduced themselves.

"Just a routine visit," George Mason quickly assured her, to calm her fears.

"In connection with...?"

"...the death of Conrad Fields," he explained.

"Please both take a seat," Celine offered, indicating two straight-back chairs set to one side, beneath the latticed window. She herself regained her seat behind a cluttered desk, striving to remain composed and professional.

"I read about it in the newspaper," she said. "It has been a terrible shock to all of us here. I had, in fact, been expecting to hear from his widow about the funeral arrangements, anticipating that people from this office might wish to attend. But I have heard nothing."

"His funeral took place last week," Mason informed her, to set her mind at ease on that score. "Were you also aware, Ms. Levasseur, that a similar attack had been made against Willem de Vries, manager of Zuider Bank, Amsterdam?"

Genuine shock and disbelief crossed the woman's not unattractive features.

"You can't be serious, Inspector Mason," she protested.

"It was almost an exact replica of what took place in the City of London," the detective continued. "An unknown gunman entered the bank soon after opening and fired point-blank at his chosen victim. Mr. de Vries is reported to be in a coma."

Celine Levasseur turned pale and looked aghast at her visitors.

"This is just terrible news, beyond belief," she gasped. "And you have no idea of a motive, or a culprit?"

"We are here in Jersey expressly for that purpose," Detective Sergeant Aubrey explained, speaking for the first time. "To further our enquiries."

"What my colleague and I need to know," Mason added, "is the precise nature of the two men's relationship with this company. We do know that they have in the past arranged for large sums of money to be transferred to your account at Sark Banking Corporation."

The office manager appeared to bridle at the veiled suggestion of wrong-doing. Recovering her poise after hearing the devastating news of de Vries' fate, which had not been covered by the Jersey press, she rose to her feet and said, quite forcefully in the circumstances:

"This is a perfectly legitimate business, Inspector Mason, and I resent any implication to the contrary."

"Calm yourself, Ms. Levasseur," the detective urged. "As I explained, this is just a routine visit. Nobody is accusing this company, or you personally, of any misdeed."

The woman settled back into her seat and returned a rather aggrieved smile.

"Mr. Fields and Mr. de Vries were both directors of this company," she then said. "They helped set it up three years ago, to take advantage of the booming property market."

"Subprime mortgages?" Alison enquired.

Celine shook her head emphatically.

"Absolutely not," she averred. "Our directors, as experienced bankers, would never have countenanced such a risky strategy. We operated at the high end of the business, advancing loans to large-scale construction projects, mainly in the leisure industry."

"Hotels, vacation centers, sports complexes. Things like that?" Mason enquired.

The woman nodded agreement.

"Didn't that sector suffer badly in the recent downturn?" Alison Aubrey asked.

"There were some notable setbacks, certainly, for many companies in the business," the woman explained. "But most of our loans have proved viable. We vet our clients very carefully beforehand."

"And the ones that didn't prove, as you put it, viable?" George Mason pressed.

"Normal mortgage company and bank practice, which we also adhere to, would be foreclosure, followed by repossession. We have, in fact, foreclosed on only two developments over the past twelve months."

"Which would those be?"

Celine Levasseur reached down into a lower drawer of her desk and withdrew two files, which she passed across to her visitors. She then made coffee, allowing the two detectives time to peruse the material and get the feel of Alderney's high-end mortgage business. As coffee was served, the tension gradually dissipated and the trio chatted amiably over a range of subjects, before Mason, holding up one of the files, asked:

"What exactly is The Derwent Club?"

"It's a timeshare in the Lake District," Celine explained. "On the banks of Derwentwater, just outside the town of Keswick."

"The project collapsed?"

"Last autumn, in fact," the other explained. "After what seemed a promising start, the developer could not induce enough people to buy shares. And some prospective clients who had signed provisional agreements had to back out as the employment situation deteriorated and hedge funds tanked. By October, the developer had fallen three months behind on his loan repayments. We had no option but to repossess."

"The developer in question being this Paul Richardson listed here as residing at The Old Manse, Buttermere?" Alison enquired.

Celine concurred.

"This other failure is even more surprising," George Mason remarked, reading from the file, "in view of the amenities it offered. Nordic and downhill skiing, rock-climbing, hiking, yachting, golf, archery and falconry. How could they go wrong with a mix like that, and in America too?"

"The USA suffered at least as serious economic problems as we did," Celine countered. "Thousands of people on Wall Street lost their jobs. Since Rollrock Ridge, a development in the White Mountains of New Hampshire, boasted several financiers among its members, as well as high-profile media figures, it was adversely affected by the economic downturn. They were foreclosed last December."

"Rollrock Ridge was not just another timeshare, was it?" Alison enquired.

"It had a rather different business model," the office manager explained. "Clients purchased their own log cabins within the overall complex, which they could use for personal vacations or retirement purposes, or simply rent out. The developer intended to levy an annual maintenance fee to cover the sporting amenities and the communal areas, such as the restaurant and health spa. It was marketed as an active retirement project, a popular concept in America."

The senior detective scratched his head and looked a bit puzzled. Something didn't seem altogether- right to him, but he could not quite put his finger on it.

"The developer in question here is Walter Cornelius, of Palladine Road, Meredith?" Alison Aubrey asked.

Celine again nodded.

"Meredith is in central New Hampshire," she explained, as Alison noted down names and addresses, "close to the White Mountains."

"Sounds like a wonderful place to build a retirement complex," Alison said.

"By all accounts, it is," Celine agreed. "I myself have never visited New Hampshire, but my nephew went to a place called North Conway on a skiing trip last year. He was impressed with the wildness of the scenery."

George Mason absorbed as much information as he could from the two files, while waiting for his young colleague to finish her coffee.

"I think we have the sort of information we need for the time being," he said eventually, thanking the office manager for her assistance and rising to leave.

Celine Levasseur gave him her business card.

"Please call me if you need any further assistance," she cordially offered, as they stepped out into the street.

"What's your impression?" Mason asked his companion as, minutes later, they were strolling along Victoria Avenue, past the large yachting marina towards The Gardens of the Sea. In the distance, they heard the siren of the French ferry from Brittany, as it approached the quay.

"Celine Levasseur seems genuine enough," Alison replied. "And she seemed truly shocked on hearing about Willem de Vries."

"Odd, though, that two directors of the same company should be targets of the same assassin, and within such a short space of time. Were you aware that the two incidents were exactly two weeks apart?"

"It hadn't occurred to me," Alison admitted.

"Both on a Friday, too," Mason remarked. "Black Friday, you might call it."

"Aren't you being a bit over-dramatic, Inspector?" she teased.

Mason raised his eyebrows at that remark, but said nothing. When they eventually reached the gardens, having spent some time admiring the variety of craft in Elizabeth Marina, he installed his colleague at a restaurant table with a view over the bay, while he located the telephone and placed a direct call to London.

"Put me through to Donald Dinwiddie," he asked the switchboard operator, on connecting with Scotland Yard.

"Inspector Mason," came the cheery response on the other end of the line. "Enjoying your jaunt to the Channel Islands?"

"Lovely weather," the detective replied. "Just about to take lunch on the seafront."

"Lucky devil," the Scot remarked. "It's raining buckets here in London."

"I followed up your lead to Alderney Mortgages. They seem a legitimate enough firm to me, quite above board. They have recently foreclosed on two major developments."

"Find out who did the property valuations before those two loans were granted," the forensic accountant advised him.

"Surely," George Mason objected, "it would be one and the same company?"

"Not necessarily," the other countered. "Some lenders often use an independent outfit, called a real estate services company, to perform the initial appraisal."

"Why would that be?" the puzzled detective wanted to know.

"It gives the client more confidence, Inspector," Dinwiddie explained, "that the valuation is fair and impartial."

"That makes sense," George Mason agreed. "I'll call them back straight away and see what they have to say."

"Contact me again if you have further queries. I'll be at my desk most of the afternoon."

"Will do," Mason promised, ringing off.

Before placing a second call, he returned to the dining-room, where Detective Sergeant Aubrey was patiently waiting for him. The long walk along the seafront had piqued her appetite. Still standing, he quickly perused the menu and said:

"Order me a ham panini, Alison, with a glass of lager. I'll rejoin you in a few minutes. We'll have a quick lunch and visit some of the sights. I just have one more call to make."

He hurried back to the foyer and dialed the number on Celine Levasseur's business card, hoping she had not already gone out to lunch. He was in luck.

"Alderney Mortgages," came the pert reply.

"Inspector George Mason here," he said. "I called by about an hour ago."

"I remember very well, Inspector. What can I do for you now?"

"Tell me, Ms. Levasseur, if your company, in addition to granting loans, also does the preliminary appraisal of the properties in question."

He thought he detected a momentary hesitation on the office manager's part, before she said:

"All initial appraisals and valuations are done for us by Chapman & Wilks, a real estate services company on the neighboring island of Guernsey. That way, our mortgage clients can be assured of impartiality."

"That is what I wished to confirm, Ms. Levasseur," the detective said. "Thank you for your assistance."

"My pleasure, Inspector," Celine said. "Chapman & Wilks are listed in the local telephone directory, if you need to contact them."

"That may be necessary, at some stage," he replied.

Replacing the receiver, he rejoined his colleague, by which time his beer had arrived. He sat down and took a large draft.

"Lunch will be here in just a few more minutes," Alison informed him. "Turn up anything useful?"

"Routine matters, mainly," he replied, non-commitally. "I think our best move now, after we return to London, is to discover as much as we can about the two foreclosed developments Celine Levasseur mentioned."

"Which do we tackle first?"

"Probably The Derwent Club," he replied. "Bill Harrington won't want to fund an expense-account trip to New England out of the current department budget, if he can avoid it. Rollrock Ridge seems a long shot anyway. I think we should look nearer home, at least initially. What did you order for lunch?"

"Tuna salad," she replied, "with vinaigrette dressing."

"Bon appétit," he said, as service arrived.

CHAPTER FOUR

"Our research department didn't turn up anything on a Walter Cornelius, of Meredith, New Hampshire," Bill Harrington informed George Mason at their conference two days later. "Which is as well since, with the budget restrictions imposed by the recession, a trip to the States would be hard to justify."

"It seems a long shot to me, in any case," his subordinate replied. "What about our other person of interest, Paul Richardson?"

"That's a different kettle of fish altogether," the Chief Inspector said, more optimistically. "Turns out he's a former member of Special Air Services, from 'C' Squadron based at Basingstoke. He took part in the siege of the Iranian Embassy in London in 1980."

George Mason gave a shrewd smile.

"So we are dealing here with a person who has advanced military training and a knowledge of weapons?"

"He retired from the S.A.S. some years ago and has since moved into the leisure industry. He seems to have tried one or two small-scale ventures, including a theme park near Ripon in the Yorkshire Dales."

"But they didn't work out?"

"I think he had mixed success," Harrington replied. "With his military background, he was a stickler for careful planning, budgetary control and staff discipline. Our sources indicate that, having taken his projects so far, he sold out to large public concerns, intending to use the proceeds for something more ambitious."

"Like The Derwent Club?" Mason observed.

"A timeshare development in the Lake District, I believe. But you may know more about that than I do."

"He got in over his head there," Mason said. "Fell behind on his loan repayments."

"Alderney Mortgages lost no time foreclosing him, did they?" Harrington wryly observed. "One would have thought that, in view of the economic situation, they might have given him a bit more time to pull things round. The Lake District is, after all, a prime vacation venue. Another few months, with summer looming, and his financial position might have been quite different."

"There's very little sentiment at mortgage firms," George Mason said, "especially these days. They're terrified of being stuck with bad loans after the subprime mess."

"Paul Richardson doesn't seem the type of man to take things lying down, either."

"But would he resort to murder?"

"It's your premise, Mason, that some person unknown developed a serious grudge against the two bankers, who were also directors of the loan company. One of them is now dead; the other still in a coma."

"So Mr. Richardson now becomes a key suspect?"

"According to my reading of the situation, he's your only suspect," the Chief Inspector testily replied. "And on the face of things, he had a motive and an expert knowledge of weapons."

"What about the two literary quotations?" Mason said. "If we can link those to him as well, we could have quite a strong case."

"Research has established that both Richardson and his wife Gwen belong to a book club in Keswick, which recently did a seminar on the poetry of Wallace Stevens."

"Most interesting," Mason mused aloud. "Yet, on the other hand, thousands of people belong to book clubs, especially in remote country areas with no theatre or cinema."

"But they're not all fans of Wallace Stevens," Harrington countered.

"You're probably right about that."

His morning coffee having arrived, the Chief Inspector reached into his desk drawer to retrieve a flask of his favorite malt whiskey. George Mason took that as a clear sign that the brief conference was over. He rose to his feet.

"You'd better get up north as soon as you can," Harrington finally said, "and find out what Paul Richardson was doing on and around March 17 and

March 31 last. Since there have been no further shootings of bank managers, I am keeping my fingers crossed that the Amsterdam incident was the last. Good heavens, Inspector, the banking industry could be in serious trouble if this sort of thing continues."

"It could provoke another financial crisis," George Mason agreed. "People would rush to sell their bank shares. Stock markets could collapse."

Back in his own office checking his accumulated mail, Mason pondered his chief's remarks. Perhaps Bill Harrington was being a little too sanguine about this unusual case, but the lead to Buttermere was certainly a useful start. He would make sure Detective Sergeant Aubrey was free of other duties tomorrow, so that they could travel together.

*

The morning of April 10 dawned fine and clear. George Mason rose early, grabbed a bowl of cereal for breakfast and left the house at just turned eight o'clock, dropping his wife Adele off at Bond Street to do some shopping, on his way to the multi-storey car park at Euston Station. Taking the lift down to the main concourse, he found Alison Aubrey, smartly dressed in a light-gray two-piece suit, waiting for him by the newspaper kiosk.

"You're bang on time," he said, cheerily greeting her.

"Didn't want to risk missing the train," she quipped, adjusting her shoulder bag as they strode towards the booking-office.

"It's the Inter-city service to Glasgow," he informed her, glancing up at the indicator for confirmation. "Departs at 9.05."

Having bought day-return tickets, they located the correct platform and were soon ensconced in second-class window seats. It left on schedule and was soon gathering speed through the seedy tenements of North London, before breaking into open country, the young sergeant being much captivated by the colorful boats they passed on the Hertfordshire canals near Hemel Hempstead.

"Envious?" her colleague enquired.

"It seems such an idyllic existence," she wistfully replied, "living on a house-boat with no bills to pay, going wherever your fancy takes you on a fine day like this."

"And in winter?"

Alison smiled rather sheepishly.

"I suppose you just hunker down," she replied, "like everyone else does. Find a convenient mooring and spend your evenings in some cosy country pub."

"You're a romantic, for sure," the down-to-earth detective chided. "Perhaps you'll be able to realize your ambition one day."

"Oh, it's just a dream, George," she sighed. "I know it's not for real."

When the refreshment trolley trundled by, they bought fresh coffee and settled into their respective reading matter, glancing occasionally at points of interest beyond the carriage window.

Four hours later, the express train pulled slowly into Penrith Station, where they alighted and took the local bus service to Buttermere. The vehicle set them down just short of the parish church, facing which, on the other side of the road, was The Old Manse.

"This would be where the rector lived in the old days, wouldn't it?" Alison asked, glancing at the two-storey stone building fronted by a low wall, privet hedge and wrought-iron gate.

"He or she now probably lives in a modern apartment in Keswick," George Mason observed. "Old houses like this are expensive to maintain on receipts from dwindling congregations."

They passed through the gate, approached the front door and rang the bell. After a short interval, an attractive brunette, whom Mason estimated to be in her late forties, appeared in the open doorway.

"Inspector Mason, from Scotland Yard," he said, introducing himself. "And this is Detective Sergeant Aubrey."

As he had not forewarned the couple of his arrival, counting on the element of surprise, a puzzled Anne Richardson stared blankly back at them.

"Do please step inside," she said after a few moments, recovering her poise. "To what do I owe this dubious honor?"

She led the way into a large sitting-room, amply furnished, with chintz chair covers and matching curtains. Switching off the television set, she invited them to sit.

"We're conducting an investigation," Mason explained, "which we hope your husband can assist us with."

A look of alarm spread across the woman's taut features. With a nervous laugh, she asked:

"What sort of investigation do you mean, Inspector? And in what way could my husband Paul possibly be of assistance?"

"Is your husband at home?" the detective asked, side-stepping her question.

"I am afraid not," she replied. "Paul is returning from a business trip. I expect him back late this evening."

"Then perhaps you yourself can help us," Mason suggested.

"In whatever way I can," Anne Richardson complaisantly replied.

"Were you and your husband involved in a timeshare venture recently?" he asked.

"You are referring, no doubt, to The Derwent Club?"

"I believe that was its name."

The woman gave a heavy sigh and regretfully shook her head.

"Paul had set such store by it," she explained. "He sold out his other business interests at a modest profit and we decided to enter the timeshare field. It turned out to have been the wrong moment, unfortunately."

"You mean the near-collapse of the loan industry?" Alison Aubrey asked.

"That, and the subsequent recession," Anne replied. "The Derwent Club got off to a good start. We purchased a site on the far side of the lake, with plans for a yachting marina, a nine-hole golf course, fell-walking and stabling for horses. We also planned to install a gourmet restaurant and spa, complete with swimming pool, sauna and therapeutic massage."

"It sounds most appealing," George Mason remarked, picturing it to himself.

"We both thought it was a great idea, especially as there are few similar developments in the Lake District, owing to planning restrictions, environmentalist objections, and the like."

"Your prospective buyers had to pull out?" Alison asked.

"After they lost their jobs and their investments went south, some clients had no other option," the woman explained. "If only the lender had given us a little more time to make up the arrears, say until the end of summer, I think we might have pulled through, touch-and-go."

That remark reminded George Mason of something Bill Harrington had said.

"Do you think the lender was a little hasty in foreclosing?" he asked.

"Paul was furious with them at the time," Anne replied. "We remonstrated with them, of course, but there was nothing we could do to change their decision. As you yourself know, banks became very reluctant to lend any money at all, and mortgage companies were terrified of being stuck with non-performing loans."

"How did your husband react to the foreclosure?" Mason then asked.

"He is still brooding over it," she admitted. "We lost a deal of money, but we still have just enough to invest in one of the smaller Lakeland hotels. In fact, we're conducting an active search currently, while investment property prices are depressed."

"Is that where Paul is now," Alison asked, "out viewing prospects?"

Anne Richardson shook her head.

"My husband is out of the country at present," she said, "pursuing one of his several business interests."

"In the property field?" Mason asked.

"Er...no," came the quick reply. "Paul has developed a few sidelines related to his military career. He served in the S.A.S., you know, with considerable distinction."

"What kind of sidelines?" the detective pressed.

The woman returned an ingenuous look.

"He never talks much about them," she explained, "so I don't ask. I gather that it's all hush-hush, to do with classified military matters."

"I have a search warrant with me," the detective then said. "I should like to visit your husband's private office."

Anne Richardson's attractive features registered alarm.

"You can't be suspecting him of something illegal, can you?" she nervously asked.

"Just routine at this stage, I assure you, Mrs. Richardson," came the non-committal reply.

"Paul does not really maintain an office at home," she informed him. "He works mainly out of his briefcase, which he generally takes with him."

"But surely," Mason protested, "he has a desk or filing cabinets of some kind?"

"Step this way," she said, rising from the sofa and leading the way to a small room towards the rear of the house, where she indicated a desk in fading teak. "He positioned it to give a good view over the garden and he uses it mainly for correspondence."

"No computer?" the surprised detective remarked, glancing through the window onto an expanse of lawn fringed by budding fruit trees and straggly floral borders. One of the Lakeland peaks, which he thought might be Scafell, loomed in the background.

Anne Richardson smiled for the first time.

"Paul has no use for one," she said. "His business methods may be a little more traditional than most, but he prefers it that way. Decidedly old-school, in fact."

George Mason was disappointed. A computer hard-drive could reveal volumes of useful information. He opened the desk drawers and quickly sifted the contents, which seemed mainly to concern the aborted timeshare project. He cast his eye over correspondence from Alderney Mortgages, noting the names Conrad Fields and Willem de Vries listed as directors on the letterhead. Near the bottom of the pile, he found a different type of letter, which he immediately passed to his young colleague.

"Mueller & Wolf," she read aloud, "of Wurzburg and Kassel. I wonder what sort of firm that is?"

"Paul never mentioned contacts with Germany to me," an equally mystified Anne Richardson remarked.

"The name rings a bell," Mason said, "but I can't just recall the connection. Our research department will soon unearth it."

"This letter," Alison continued, "is to set up a meeting between your husband and one of their agents in Amsterdam."

She glanced closely at the other woman, to gauge her reaction.

"Paul did take a trip to Holland late last month," she said. "He was there three days."

"Do you recall the exact date he left England?" George Mason asked.

"Now, let me see," the woman replied, crossing to the kitchen to consult a wall calendar. "He left home by car on March 29, drove down to Banbury, Oxfordshire to stay overnight with Colin Devey, a former S.A.S. colleague. He would have continued on to Heathrow Airport the following day, which would be March 30."

"Your husband seems to be away from home quite frequently, Mrs. Richardson."

"In recent months, more often than usual," she replied.

"Was he by any chance in London around the middle of last month?" the detective wanted to know, hoping to establish a link to Conrad Fields.

"He may well have been. He visits London quite often, sometimes on business, sometimes for pleasure. S.A.S. veterans have regular reunions there, at the Army and Navy Club."

"But specifically last month?" Mason pressed.

"You will have to ask him that personally," she replied. "I was in Edinburgh during the last two weeks of March, visiting my sister. She has been a little unwell recently, recovering from an operation."

"I'm sorry to hear that," the detective said, pocketing the German letter and crossing towards the door. "I hope she soon recovers."

"One of those age-related conditions," Anne said, with a thin smile, without offering details.

"Tell me, Mrs. Richardson," Alison said, as the Scotland Yard pair were on the point of leaving, "about your husband's interest in Wallace Stevens."

"Wallace Stevens!" the other exclaimed, breaking into a surprised laugh. "You mean the famous American poet? Why, our book club did a seminar on him only a short while ago. What a curious coincidence that you should bring his name up!"

"Did you and your husband both attend the seminar?"

"I went alone on that occasion, mainly to please our president, Dotty Greenhalgh. Paul does not have much time for poets, with perhaps the exception of Rudyard Kipling. He's always been the man of action, I'm sure you understand."

The two detectives exchanged ironic glances at that rather interesting snippet of information, thanked the woman for her assistance and promised to be in touch later. Once outside, they had ample time to admire the neo-Gothic lines of the parish church of St. Kentigern, as they stood waiting for the return bus to Penrith.

*

When the Glasgow-London express train pulled into Penrith Station, they boarded smartly, hoping to secure seats in the dining car, which would have quickly filled with passengers on the long trip from Scotland. They were in luck, occupying two of the few remaining places. George Mason particularly enjoyed railway dining; a three-course meal helped pass the journey in an agreeable manner.

"Dover sole looks good to me," he remarked, scanning the menu.

Alison Aubrey took a little longer to make up her mind, as the train picked up speed towards Lancaster.

"I think I'll settle for the tournedos," she said, eventually. "Haven't had a good steak in ages."

"What do you make of our visit to The Old Manse?" he asked, after the waiter had taken their orders.

"Anne Richardson seems genuine enough," she thought, "but doesn't seem to have much idea of her husband's affairs."

"Some wives don't," Mason airily replied. "But I think we may be on to something with the ex-S.A.S. man. We now need to find out exactly what he was doing in Amsterdam on March 31. It suddenly struck me on the way from Buttermere where I had come across the name Mueller & Wolf before."

"Oh?"

"If I am not mistaken, they have something to do with weaponry."

"That's rather interesting," his young colleague remarked. "Richardson would have the means as well as a motive for the killings. That timeshare project evidently meant a great deal to him."

"But was it sufficient motive to attack two bank managers?"

"If he felt that they had done wrong by him in some way, I think it might. People have killed for much less than that."

"On the face of it," Mason said, adding a touch of fresh lemon to his sole fillet, "it seems like a fairly straightforward case of foreclosure. Unless we can prove there was some element of wrong-doing -

fraud, if you like – we could be on very uncertain ground."

Alison ordered a glass of Malbec and concentrated on her meal for a while, distracted by the sudden buzz of activity in the dining-car. Desserts were being served by the waiters and the volume of conversation had increased.

"Alderney Mortgages lost little time in serving the foreclosure notice," she eventually observed. "Perhaps that is one area we could take a closer look at."

"You may well be right," her colleague replied, impressed at her acumen. "It's something we should get our forensic accountant, Donald Dinwiddie, to look into. But it would not be my immediate priority."

"What would that be then?" a rather surprised Alison asked, between sips of her tepid, Argentine wine.

"I intend first of all to contact Messrs. Mueller & Wolf. I should then like to interview Paul Richardson in person, as someone of considerable interest in this case."

CHAPTER FIVE

"Your hunch was correct," Chief Inspector Bill Harrington told George Mason, when they met two days later for their routine conference. "Research has identified Mueller & Wolf as a manufacturer of small arms, based in Wurzburg and Kassel."

"Kassel is in the Saarland," George Mason observed, recalling a visit he had once made to that scenic area in connection with a case involving a former Stasi agent. "Do you want me to go over there?"

"That, fortunately, will not be necessary," Harrington replied. "As luck would have it, their sales manager, Ludwig Koch, is in London at this moment attending an exhibition of sporting pieces at Earls Court. He has agreed to meet with you after the morning session."

"At the Exhibition Hall?" a dubious Mason enquired.

The senior man shook his head, dismissively.

"He will be taking lunch at The King's Head, a pub on Earls Court Road directly opposite the Underground station. He has invited you to join him there at 12.30 p.m. Once you've cleared your deskwork — I need your report on Buttermere -

you'd better get over there promptly and find out what he has to say."

"I'm hoping he'll be able to throw some light on Paul Richardson's presence in Amsterdam on the day Willem de Vries was attacked."

"So you've already established that the ex-S.A.S. man was in the Dutch capital on March 31? Good work, Inspector. And, by the way, the latest news from Holland is that the bank manager remains in a coma, but there is some hope of his recovery."

George Mason heaved a sigh of relief.

"That's encouraging," he said. "Anne Richardson was able to confirm her husband's movements around that time. He's apparently away from home quite a lot these days, on what she seems to regard as confidential military matters stemming from his contacts in Special Air Services."

"Write it all up in your report, Mason," Harrington said, rather brusquely. "I have a meeting with the Superintendent at ten o'clock. It's five minutes to, already."

Mason took the none-too-subtle hint and returned to his own office, where he placed an internal call to Donald Dinwiddie, asking him to look into the spate of recent property foreclosures going through the courts, to see if he could detect a pattern of malpractise. He then placed an outside call to Buttermere, in the expectation that Paul Richardson had by now returned.

Anne Richardson, answering, appeared rather agitated.

"No, Inspector Mason," she informed him. "My husband is not back yet, and I have had no word from him. I really am concerned."

"He was due back two days ago, wasn't he?" the detective asked.

"Exactly. I would have expected him to ring, to say if he had been delayed."

"Sorry about that," Mason said. "I was hoping to speak with him."

"I'll let you know, Inspector," she promised, "the moment he arrives."

"That's most helpful of you, Anne," he replied.

Replacing the receiver, he set about clearing the backlog of correspondence that had stacked up in the last few days, before penning his report on Buttermere. By the time he had finished, it was just turned eleven o'clock. Gathering his case notes together, he placed them in his briefcase and left the office, after dropping his report on his chief's desk. He crossed the busy thoroughfare to Westminster Underground, to board the District Line to Earls Court. Once there, he soon located The King's Head, named for the beheading of Charles 1 in 1649. Aware that he was a little early, he went straight to the bar and ordered himself a pint of bitter, exchanging small talk with the barman and his immediate neighbor, who had all the marks of a pub regular. George Mason knew the type. Perched on a bar-stool with a glass in front of them, they were always on the look-out for someone – it did not much matter whom – to pass the time of day with. After a while, a short, stocky gentleman approached Mason from behind. The detective turned, to find a middle-aged gentleman with thinning hair, clad in traditional Bavarian style, complete with lederhosen. Somewhat surprised at his unconventional attire, he slipped off his stool to greet him.

"Inspector Mason?" the man enquired, offering his hand.

The detective wondered how the man had singled him out so quickly in a crowded pub, before recalling that policemen had a certain giveaway aura. He also asked himself why Ludwig Koch looked like someone you might meet any day of the week in Garmisch-Partenkirchen, but hardly in the center of London. The visitor noted the veiled look of surprise and quickly introduced himself.

"Traditional dress is something we make a point of wearing," he explained, "when representing our company at international events."

"It must arouse a deal of interest, Herr Koch," Mason observed. "And it's probably a very good sales plug, too."

"Exactly so," the Bavarian agreed, leading the detective to a table in a quiet alcove. "We are having our best year ever, so far, especially in the export market."

"What precisely are you promoting?"

"Mueller & Wolf's main line is in fowling pieces, for sports' purposes," Koch explained. "The Earls Court exhibition this week takes place annually, ahead of the Glorious Twelfth and similar, less prominent, sporting events throughout the UK."

"Grouse shooting?" the detective remarked, with raised eyebrows, unsure whether he approved of shooting birds for sport. "Never tried it myself. The closest I came was with clay pigeons as a rookie constable at Epping."

"We cater for that, too," the other enthusiastically remarked, half hoping he had found a customer.

George Mason, however, was at this point more interested in food. Encouraged by his unconventional host to order whatever he wished, he said, after a brief glance at the menu:

"I should think the game pie, a specialty of the house, might be appropriate to the occasion."

The German did not detect the slight note of irony in his guest's voice. He cordially approved the choice and followed suit.

"I think a Mosel riesling would do it justice," he proposed, summoning the waiter.

"I expect you get to travel quite a lot in your line of work," Mason then said.

"We cover several events in the course of the year," Koch explained, "split between myself and my assistant manager. We go less often to America nowadays. Hunting has been on the decline there in recent years."

"How about Holland?"

"I was there only last month," Koch replied, in some surprise. "Mainly to promote our latest line, the Mueller & Wolf K39 machine-pistol."

"What kind of weapon would that be?" a curious George Mason asked.

"It's a magazine-fed, fully automatic hand gun."

"A bit extreme for fowling purposes, isn't it?" came the retort, as the waiter poured the chilled Mosel.

Ludwig Koch broke into a laugh.

"You have a nice sense of irony, Inspector," he said. "I appreciate it. The K39 is not, of course, designed for sporting purposes. We developed it to fill a niche in personnel defense."

"Can you elaborate on that?"

"Late last month," the other explained, "the Defense Minister of the North African Republic was in Amsterdam on official business. We met with him to discuss its potential for the N.A.R.'s presidential bodyguard. As a result of that meeting, which was necessarily brief for lack of time, he invited us to send an agent over to Africa to give demonstrations."

"That agent wouldn't by any chance be a certain Paul Richardson, would it?" Mason asked, putting two and two together.

The salesman's jaw dropped. How could this London policeman have become party to such a confidential business matter, he seemed to be asking himself?

"Why...yes... it was, as a matter of fact," he stammered. "Richardson was recommended to us through a third party here in London, on the basis of his record with Special Air Services."

"And the meeting took place on March 31?"

Ludwig Koch, even more surprised, nodded in agreement, with the uneasy feeling that he may have somehow fallen foul of the law, in some inexplicable way.

"It was all perfectly legitimate," he hastened to explain. "We have already applied to the German government for an export license, should the deal go through."

"I don't doubt that," George Mason assured him.

At that juncture, the game pie arrived, served with baked potato and endive salad. The serious business of eating occupied their full attention for the next several minutes, Mason noting with pleasure that his host tackled the typically English dish with gusto. Germans do like their food, he reflected.

"Was it a morning or afternoon meeting, in Amsterdam?" he eventually asked.

"Mid-morning, at the Republic's Consulate," came the reply. "By the way, Inspector, that was an excellent choice of fare."

"Glad you approve," the detective said, refilling their wine glasses, while reflecting that Richardson would have had ample time before the meeting to enter Zuider Bank. He wondered if Herr Koch was aware of the incident, but decided not to press the point.

"Has Richardson contacted you yet regarding the success of his mission?" he asked.

The salesman's face clouded a little, as he nudged the remains of his satisfying meal aside.

"I am afraid not," he replied. "To tell you the truth, Inspector, I was expecting him to show up here at Earls Court this very day. There could, quite understandably, have been some delay in his travel arrangements."

"Of course, Herr Koch," the detective agreed. "He is only a couple of days behind schedule, but his wife Anne seemed rather concerned, partly because he has not even telephoned her."

"I fully expect to meet him here in London before the week is out."

"I need a word with him, too," Mason said, "regarding a matter related to his recent doings in Amsterdam."

"He's not in trouble with the law, is he?" his now anxious-looking luncheon host asked, mulling thoughts of diamond smuggling, drug dealing and the like. "We did a thorough background check, as we invariably do when hiring agents. The sensitive nature of our business, you understand?"

"Our enquiries are purely routine, at this point," the detective assured him, handing him his calling card. "Do please contact me as soon as Richardson re-surfaces."

*

On the morning Milovan Piric was due to check out of his hotel at Hoorn, he received a telegram from Jason requesting a meeting in Hamburg. As he sat gazing at the uneventful coastal scenery on the mid-morning service from Amsterdam Centraal, having taken the first available train back to the Dutch capital, he mulled over the possible reasons for this sudden change of plan. He had fully expected to make his way gradually into Scandinavia and receive his next instructions poste restante at The Old Post Office, Stockholm. The worst complexion he could put on it was that Jason had decided to call the whole thing off. Or it could simply mean that there were to be minor adjustments to the overall project. Why then, he wondered, was his contact coming out into the open again, when he could easily have given instructions by mail?

The uncertainty continued to nag him as, on eventual arrival at Hamburg Hauptbahnhof, he deposited his suitcase in a left-luggage locker and, noting that he was almost an hour ahead of schedule, crossed to the food kiosk to buy bratwurst for a quick lunch. Having eaten, a quick visit to the bookstalls to glimpse the headlines of foreign newspapers, particularly De Telegraaf, assured him that the heat was off regarding the incident at Zuider Bank. He left the station and strode confidently down the Ballindamm by the River Elbe, in the direction of the Altstadt, the historic heart of the old port city. Not having visited

Hamburg before, but aware from newsreels of its wartime devastation, he was struck by the elegant shops, broad boulevards and general air of prosperity. As in Dresden, which he had made a detour to visit on making his escape westwards from the fatal hold-up in Debrecen, the city fathers had set about restoring it to its pre-war ambience. Milovan Piric was a man who appreciated the finer points of architecture, having spent part of his military service as a security guard at several national monuments in and around Belgrade.

The man he knew only as Jason was waiting for him, as pre-arranged, at a small bar near the Hammaburg, the site of the fortified residence of medieval German bishops.

"It was the base for missionary forays into Denmark and Sweden," Jason informed him, noting with some surprise the other's interest in the landmark, "from the ninth century onwards."

"That should make it the oldest part of Hamburg," the Serb suggested.

"Indeed, it is," the other replied, "according to my guidebook. Now, history aside, I suppose you are wondering why I summoned you here at such short notice?"

The hired assassin nodded, but said nothing.

"You've slipped up a little, Milovan," Jason then said, rather acidly.

The Serb's eyes opened wide in disbelief. He took a draft of his pilsner and awaited further explanation, unsure if this wasn't some ruse on the other's part to avoid fulfilling his part of the bargain; to wit, paying the agreed fee.

"Willem de Vries is not dead," Jason said, giving his words time to sink in, before adding: "He is lying in a coma at the Royal Hospital, Amsterdam."

Piric's eyes narrowed.

"What makes you so sure of that?" he challenged.

"There was a brief item on a television news channel recently," Jason said. "Quite by chance, I switched it on in my hotel room; otherwise, I would not have been aware of the fact. If I understood the German language correctly, there's a chance, albeit a slim one, that he will recover."

The Serb did not know where to look. Avoiding direct eye-contact with his interlocutor, he shifted his feet uneasily.

"And you are seeking partial repayment of the fee?" he asked, eventually.

"I am seeking fulfillment of your contract," Jason snapped back. "You are going to have to return to Amsterdam and finish the job, without delay. If de Vries recovers, he may well be able to help the police come up with a motive, together with a description of the perpetrator. Which, of course, means you, my dear friend."

Milovan Piric returned a wry smile. Jason made it all sound so simple; yet he realized that it had to be done.

"Do you have another note for me to leave at the scene?" he enquired, with heavy irony.

Jason shook his head, emphatically.

"What is the purpose," the Serb then asked, "of these arcane literary references?"

The other smiled for the first time, his expression conveying as much cynicism as humor.

"Let us simply say," he replied, "that I am indulging a personal whim and leave it at that. But at the same time, it could be regarded as a form of taunt to the police."

"You mean that you are dropping a type of clue that some gumshoe cannot for the life of him figure out, so that he will waste hours of his precious time?"

"Clever, don't you think?" Jason remarked, beaming self-satisfaction.

Piric wondered uneasily if his paymaster wasn't being a little too clever. He himself would never have left any form of calling card at the scene, no matter how bizarre.

"I shall return to Amsterdam at once," he announced, "and finish the job."

"Enter the hospital during routine visiting hours," the other advised. "You'll be less conspicuous then. And don't make any mistakes!"

*

Milovan Piric drained his pilsner and left the bar, declining an offer of lunch since he had already snacked at the railway station. He retraced his steps through the Altstadt to the Ballindamm and continued along it until reached a large riverside park, from where he observed the freighters plying along the River Elbe towards the sea. The few people abroad were mainly mothers or grandparents with pre-school children. It suited the ex-mercenary to while away the time before the next Amsterdam train left in such an unfrequented spot, where he could enjoy the fresh breeze coming across the river while he smoked a Dutch half-corona. He felt sure that, following the events at Debrecen, Interpol would have provided European police forces with a fairly accurate portrait of him, even if several years old. An official photo was routinely taken when he first joined the army. He flattered himself that he had not aged much in the intervening years, and preferred to avoid city centers as far as he could.

It was early evening by the time he regained the Dutch capital, but nothing could have prepared him for what he encountered on leaving Centraal Station. Hundreds of people, many of them wearing orange, thronged the main square, where a brass band was playing. With some time to kill, he mingled with the crowd for a while, enjoying the music and the festive atmosphere, before venturing into the residential areas to share vicariously in the neighborhood street parties. Along the Herengracht, he encountered canal boats decked out in colored flags, a pervasive odor of beer and grilled sausages, and rock music with a DJ. People were drinking and dancing in large, uninhibited groups; everywhere, the color orange. Suspecting that it was some kind of national event, he paused at the canal-side, bought a bratwurst with lashings of mustard and spoke briefly to the vendor. He had thought something might be afoot earlier in the day, as the train from Hoorn sped past a long line of trucks entering the city, where he had found a small battalion of officials busying themselves in the public areas near the station. Only now did he learn from the vendor that the Dutch and up to a million visitors were celebrating Queen Day in honor of the country's monarch, and that this was Holland's premier festival.

That suited his purposes, he mused with satisfaction, as he hastily chewed his last mouthful of sausage and washed it down with a plastic beaker of coffee, not wishing to join in the general alcohol binge so as to remain fully alert. He then walked back in the direction of the Royal Hospital, browsing through the gaily-decked stalls of the large street market on his way. In the background, strains of an outdoor symphony orchestra could be heard, playing what he took to be Mozart. On an evening like this, the general atmosphere would be carefree and relaxed, he considered; guard would be down. Even the local police, although not drinking, could occasionally be observed smoking and chatting amicably with the locals. He gave them a wide berth, from time to time checking that his Ruger pistol was safely tucked into his shoulder holster.

The Royal Hospital also shared in the general festivities, if in more subdued style. Orange balloons and bunting were in evidence as he reached the entrance hall, and there seemed to be an event in progress for sick children in a large reception area to the left. No one paid him much attention as he joined the drift towards the main stair and ascended to the second floor, which opened into a public ward. A quick glance told him that most of the patients were sitting up in bed receiving visitors. The few that weren't so occupied were reading books or watching a television screen placed high up in the far corner of the room. It was a mixed ward, too, most of the patients being female. He spun round and headed back towards the main stair, ascending to the next level, where he hoped to find the private rooms. A patient in a coma, especially someone of Willem de Vries' status, would hardly be in a public ward. He would be alone, recumbent, unconscious and instantly recognizable.

Leaving the stairwell and turning the corner, he immediately noticed a uniformed officer positioned outside a door on the right. The officer turned his head at the sound of footfalls and, within moments, recognized the intruder and made to draw his side-arm. Milovan Piric stopped in his tracks, turned and raced back towards the stairs, leaping down them two at a time until he regained the entrance hall, aware that his pursuer would not risk firing his weapon in such a crowded area. To the consternation of the staff and visitors alike, he dashed towards the revolving main door, followed at some fifty paces by the armed guard. Once outside, he soon lost himself in the thickening throng of revelers, above which he caught the sound of piercing police whistles, but heard no shots. He fled down a side-street towards the nearest canal, then continued walking hurriedly away from the city center to join the crowd milling through the extensive street market. Any other day, he grimly reflected, and his goose would have been well and truly cooked. Police would have converged on him from all quarters and quickly apprehended him. Thank heavens, he thought, as he at length slowed down to catch his breath, that it was Queen Day; it was almost enough to turn him, a staunch republican, into a convinced monarchist.

Aware that rail and bus termini would now be closely watched, he hailed a taxi and directed it to the border town of Zwolle, where he could catch a train to Bremen, just inside Germany. It unnerved him that he had been instantly recognized at the hospital. Interpol must have re-circulated his likeness, as if they already suspected his involvement in the recent bank attacks. He would take even greater precautions in the future and, when all this business with Jason was concluded, would quit Europe for good and settle permanently in East Africa.

*

That same evening George Mason, quite unaware that they were celebrating Queen Day in

Holland, was relaxing with a glass of wine in front of the television set, while his wife Adele was preparing dinner. An item on BBC News caused him to sit bolt upright and pay close attention.

"Guess what," he called to Adele.

"The prime minister has resigned?" she asked, wiping her hands on her apron as she stepped in from the kitchen.

"No such luck," he replied, with feeling. "There's been an attempted coup d'etat in the North African Republic. The defense minister, Julius Nokubia, has been arrested along with other ringleaders, including the finance secretary."

"What's so unusual about that?" a skeptical Adele, through a faint halo of garlic, wanted to know. "That sort of thing happens all the time."

"Indeed it does," her husband replied. "But you'll never guess who has been arrested along with them."

Adele sat down on the sofa beside him for a moment and glanced at the screen. It showed a Caucasian in early middle-age, wearing what appeared to be military fatigues, glowering at the camera with a look somewhere between disgust and disbelief.

"He looks English to me," she observed.

"Great Scot, Adele!" George Mason exclaimed. "It's the very person I've been trying to trace for the last several days! He was recently introduced to Julius Nokubia at the N.A.R. consulate in

Amsterdam, by a representative of the German small arms firm, Mueller & Wolf."

"And as a result of that meeting, he traveled to North Africa?"

"Ostensibly to demonstrate a new model of magazine pistol that would fire rounds, just like a machine-gun. Ludwig Koch told me it was destined for the presidential bodyguard. Paul Richardson must have been duped and become implicated, through his contact with Nokubia, in this abortive coup d'etat."

"Poor chap," Adele remarked, returning to her cooking. "He looks completely crestfallen."

There will be a drawn-out trial, Mason thought, possibly followed by a period of imprisonment, if he cannot clear himself. The Foreign Office will get heavily involved, Koch and German lawyers will be there, and the media of course will have a field day. There was little chance that he himself would get to interview the ex-S.A.S. man, at least within the next several weeks, possibly months. He breathed a heavy sigh, switched the television off, sat back and nursed his glass of supermarket merlot philosophically, as the aroma of spaghetti carbonara wafted through from the kitchen. A few minutes later, Adele reappeared.

"Open a fresh bottle of red, will you, George, and pour me about half a glass? Dinner's almost on."

CHAPTER SIX

"So your Special Air Services man is now hors de combat, in a manner of speaking, according to what you've just told me?" Chief Inspector Bill Harrington quipped, glancing pointedly across the cluttered desk at his subordinate during their morning conference two days later. "Mind you, Inspector, I watched the same news program myself, but the significance of that particular item hadn't registered."

"He's currently being held in custody at M'bala," Mason ruefully admitted. "I contacted the Foreign Office yesterday and there seems to be little prospect of bail being granted, at least not in the immediate future."

Bill Harrington noisily cleared his throat and reached down to the lower drawer of his desk for his bottle of single malt, placing it ostentatiously on his desk without pouring it. He would wait until his morning coffee arrived, to chase one with the other.

"Does his wife know about this?" he then asked.

"I checked with her yesterday. She hadn't seen the BBC announcement and, quite naturally, she was extremely upset. She's planning to fly out there in a day or two."

"And you are left without a suspect in the bank murders?"

"Paul Richardson must be put on hold for the time being," Mason replied. "A pity, because I had already established that he was in Amsterdam the very day Willem de Vries was shot."

The Chief Inspector pursed his lips and slowly shook his head, as if in commiseration.

"But being George Mason," he said, with a subtle touch of irony, "you doubtless have other arrows in your quiver?"

"It would mean a trip across the Atlantic."

"You are referring to that other individual you mentioned some days ago?"

"Cornelius," Mason said. "Walter Cornelius, to be precise. His leisure development in the White Mountains was also foreclosed by that Channel Islands firm I visited, Alderney Mortgages."

"Of which Conrad Fields and Willem de Vries were both directors?"

"Exactly."

Harrington's eyes narrowed slightly and his hand moved vaguely towards the whiskey bottle, but withdrew. Mason sat there expectantly, knowing full well that the Chief Inspector was weighing up the cost/effectiveness ratio, following recent cuts in the departmental budget.

"Commissioner Manwaring will have the final say on this," he said. "I'll make out the best case I can for you, George, but it may mean that you will have to defer this case until Richardson is sprung from jail."

"What really concerns me, Chief Inspector," his colleague then said, "is to get to the bottom of this business before any more bank managers are targeted."

"Not the most popular species these days, are they?" Harrington quipped. "But that's no reason to gun them down in broad daylight. What strikes me is the boldness of the way these attacks were carried out. It's a professional job all right."

"You mean someone employed a hit-man?"

"Does it seem to you like the handiwork of some disgruntled mortgage client?"

"Richardson, however, is professionally trained," George Mason came back, to justify his own point of view.

"You may well be correct, Inspector, but I would keep an open mind."

"We're looking for someone with literary proclivities, too," Mason said. "Someone well up in modern literature, judging by the quotation left at the scene of each crime."

"Then you've got your work cut out for you, haven't you? The best of British luck!"

"I've a feeling I'm going to need it," his colleague said, rising to return to routine administrative chores.

*

Three days later, George Mason was sitting in a British Airways Airbus approaching Logan Airport. It had taken the intervening time to set up liaison with the New Hampshire State Police, and the detective was hoping the delay would not be critical. The flight across the Atlantic had been smooth and uneventful. His young colleague had passed the time reading a historical novel; while he just barely completed the Times crossword and read the Business Section, to check his small portfolio of stocks. At Boston they transferred to the shuttle service to Manchester, where they were to be met by Captain Ivor Wells.

"Amazing that Bill Harrington detailed you for this trip, Alison," he remarked, when the short flight was well under way, "in view of budget restraints."

"I was agreeably surprised, too," the Detective Sergeant admitted. "Apparently, Commissioner Manwaring thought it would be good experience, and I was hardly going to turn down an opportunity like this."

"Professional development, it's called."

"Call it what you like, George. I am really looking forward to it, especially if your hunch is correct and we can make real progress in the case."

"It remains to be seen, Alison, whether this trip bears fruit or not. But at least we'll get a change of scenery and some fresh mountain air. Don't you sometimes tire of the metropolis and its traffic fumes?"

Alison kept a diplomatic silence on that score: how could she complain about working in London when it had meant a key promotion early in her career?

"When are we due to land?" she asked, instead.

"Any time now," her colleague replied. "Manchester is only about fifty miles north of Boston."

Hardly had he finished speaking when the nose of the small aircraft dipped, to begin its short descent. After touch-down, they emerged from the airport building with their overnight luggage, to be greeted by Captain Wells. Standing by the exit, he was instantly recognizable in his dark-blue uniform, as he strode forward to greet them, his hand outstretched.

"Welcome to New Hampshire, Inspector Mason," he said. "This your first visit?"

George Mason clasped his hand, wincing slightly at the firmness of the other's grip, and nodded.

"By the way," he said, "this is my colleague, Detective Sergeant Alison Aubrey."

"Pleased to meet you, ma'am," the officer said, lightly grasping her hand in turn. "My car is waiting outside."

He took their luggage and placed it in the trunk before ushering them into the rear seat of his Ford sedan. Communicating briefly with HQ, he spun the car out of the parking lot and was soon speeding northwards on Interstate 93, conversing over his shoulder as they went.

"This person of interest, your Walter Cornelius," he remarked, "does not appear in police records anywhere in the United States. In short, he appears to be clean as a whistle."

"Have you managed to locate him?" Mason asked, expectantly.

"That's a good question, Inspector," the other said. "I ascertained that he maintains a place called Lakeview, on Palladine Road, Meredith, and is up-to-date with his property taxes. I've tried several times to contact him by telephone, without success."

That said, the American concentrated on his driving as the traffic intensified around Concord, the state capital. Once north of there, the Scotland Yard pair sat back in their seats to take in the novel surroundings, noting the vast tracts of mixed forest either hand, the new leaf-buds of the birches and maples contrasting with the darker conifers. Leaving Interstate 93 at Tilton, they proceeded at a restricted speed on the winding road alongside a broad expanse of water, in places fringed with wooden cabins awaiting summer rental.

"Lake Winnisquam," Captain Wells explained. "It's one of several large lakes in this area. Looks very quiet now, but it will come into its own in a few weeks' time."

"Vacationers rent these little cabins?" a curious George Mason asked. "For what purpose?"

"Power boating mainly," came the reply. "Fishing is also quite popular, or you can hire jet-skis, kayaks, whatever."

"It looks very appealing," Alison Aubrey remarked.

"It is, ma'am, I can assure you. Even more so when the trees come fully into leaf. We're very proud of the Granite State."

Within another thirty minutes, they had reached Meredith. Captain Wells pulled up outside the Ashland Hotel, which they had pre-booked on the internet. It was a trim, family-run establishment just off the main center of what appeared to be a small market town. The Captain helped carry their luggage through to Reception.

"I expect you'll be wanting to rest up a while and grab a bite to eat after your journey," he said. "I've got routine business in Holderness, five miles north of here, so I may as well kill two birds with one stone. I'll call back for you in two hours' time. It'll be about three o'clock."

"That suits me just fine," Alison remarked, the moment he had left. "I aim to take a short nap and then freshen up."

George Mason, on completing registration, led the way upstairs and soon located their adjacent rooms on the second floor. They were comfortably furnished, he noted, with windows overlooking the parking lot of a colonial-era Baptist church.

"I'll expect you down in about an hour's time," he told Alison, as he entered his own room to take a quick shower. It concerned him a little that Captain Wells had been unable to contact Walter Cornelius, and he was hoping they would have more success when they called at his address later that afternoon.

On changing into lighter clothes for the warm May weather, he left the hotel to explore his new environs. Meredith consisted of a single main street, along which he noted a public library, a post office, an antique shop, a Civil War memorial and several small businesses, including a bookstore, a realtor and a tobacconist. It was one of the most compact and picturesque towns he had ever visited, all amenities being within a few minutes' walk. The population, he mused, could hardly be more than a few thousand souls. They seemed a hardy, outgoing people, some of whom greeted him cordially on the sidewalks even though he was a complete stranger. Stepping inside the bookstore, he immediately noticed a rack of colored brochures advertising tourist attractions such as The Loon Center and Castle in the Clouds, various potteries, art galleries, craft centers and a wildlife park claiming black bears, cougars and bobcats among its denizens. His curiosity aroused, he delved deeper and came up, much intrigued, with a brochure for Rollrock Ridge. On leaving the store, he espied an Italian coffee bar called Luigi's nearby, dropped in, ordered a cappuccino and leafed through the document.

He discovered that it was situated on rising ground to the east of Waterville Valley, perhaps some thirty miles north of Meredith. Closer inspection revealed that the brochure was more in the nature of a prospectus for an as-yet-incomplete resort development. The central feature was a luxury hotel open to the general public, offering gourmet dining and a spa. Dispersed throughout the extensive grounds were chalets that could be purchased only by accredited members of Rollrock Ridge Club. A surprising feature, to the detective's mind, was that the chalets could be occupied by their owners for a maximum of three months per year; for the remaining time, they were to be rented out to the public, the owner retaining half the rental income. Mason glanced up from his reading, momentarily distracted by travel posters on the wall showing views of Lake Como. He also noticed, in a display case just below the bar, a tempting array of Italian pastries. Should he, or shouldn't he? A glance at his watch told him it was almost time to call back for his colleague; he would postpone his appetite until then.

"How do you like this for a spell of fine spring weather?" he asked her, as she stepped out of the hotel clad in a print frock and loose cardigan.

"I'm not complaining," she replied. "On the television news in my room, it showed heavy rain in London."

He led her down one of several side-streets descending steeply to the lake. Crossing over busy Route 3, the main artery northwards, they found themselves in an attractive park extending to the water's edge, where mallards and mew gulls were pestering the picnickers. Following directions given him by the hotel receptionist, they proceeded along the boardwalk to an outdoor restaurant called The Beach Garden.

"Why, they even serve fish-and-chips," he jocularly remarked, on scanning the menu. "Who would have thought that?"

"It's become one of those universal dishes," laughed Alison, "like pizza and hamburger. It wouldn't surprise me if you could order it in Peking. I'm opting for something light, like the prawn salad. Servings here are said to be much more generous than in England."

"We'll certainly put that theory to the test," her companion replied, ordering pizza.

The tables, right up against the water's edge, were about half-occupied. Young waitresses in brief denim shorts wove among them ferrying plates of food and iced drinks. Dogs peered expectantly at their owners. Gulls wheeled raucously overhead.

"I could spend quality time here," Alison remarked, gazing wistfully across the vast lake towards the distant mountains.

"Certainly has its attractions," her colleague agreed, tucking in the moment his pizza arrived. "And guess what? I picked up a brochure on Rollrock Ridge at the local bookstore. It's not all that far from here."

"What's it all about?" Alison eagerly enquired.

"To be honest," he replied, "I don't even know if it's still viable….with the foreclosure, I mean. They advertise it as a sort of year-round vacation club, focusing on keep-fit and outdoor pursuits. There's both Nordic and downhill skiing in winter; yachting, cycling, hiking and falconry in the summer. Can't imagine how it could fail, it's such an appealing proposition."

"The economic downturn, in my view," Alison considered. "Prospective buyers, such as lawyers, financiers and CEOs, have also suffered heavy losses. I imagine that many of those who signed contracts initially have had to pull out, for one reason or another, leaving the developer high and dry."

"The elusive Mr. Cornelius, no less," Mason remarked. "If we get to interview him, we shall soon find out what went wrong. He would have forfeited a great deal of money if the place was repossessed by Alderney Mortgages."

"He may feel, too, like Paul Richardson, that his backers were too quick to pull the plug. He would probably feel highly resentful and hard done by."

"But would he commit murder?"

"That is the unanswered question, Alison. I should also like to know something of his literary tastes."

"Wallace Stevens again?"

"Interesting you should mention that. I glanced at a volume of his poetry in the hotel lounge, where they have an interesting selection of books."

"Out of curiosity, George?"

"I was hoping to come across the quote that was left at the Amsterdam crime scene."

"Money is a kind of poetry?" Alison asked, with raised eyebrows. "Did you have any luck?"

"I did not, unfortunately. But I did come across some very original writing. How about Thirteen Ways of Looking at a Blackbird, for example?"

"Or The Emperor of Ice Cream?" Alison came back at once.

"I recall now," Mason said, impressed, "that you studied him at college."

"He was always one of my favorites. He and G.M. Hopkins. That quotation most likely came from an essay. It doesn't have the ring of poetry, not to my ears, at any rate."

"I'll defer to your superior judgment on that," George Mason gallantly conceded, forking his last mouthful of pizza as his colleague toyed with the remnants of her prawn salad.

*

After their al fresco lunch, they strolled back along the boardwalk towards their hotel, pausing to watch a large passenger vessel, the Mt. Washington, approach the quay and take on trippers for the afternoon voyage. It was still early in the season and the boat would be lucky, Mason considered, if it left half-full, many of the passengers being groups of retirees arriving by chartered bus from neighboring Vermont and Massachusetts. They found Captain Ivor Wells sitting in his squad car waiting for them outside the

Ashland Hotel, and the trio were soon heading south away from the lake towards Palladine Road. Within minutes, they had stopped on a rise giving stunning views of the mountains and of a smaller lake below them, gleaming in the sunlight. Leaving the car, they approached an isolated residence set well back from the road and partly screened by towering pine-trees.

"Seems very quiet to me," the American officer remarked, pressing the doorbell and stepping back to survey the property. There being no response, he tried again.

"The place looks deserted," George Mason observed.

"Which would explain why I haven't been able to reach him by telephone," the Captain said, as they returned to the car. "Many older residents winterize their homes, shut them down and move to Florida for the duration. Snowbirds, we call them."

"Like a migrating species," Alison Aubrey put in, much taken with the idea.

"Most of them are back by Easter," the Captain informed her, "but some may linger on until well into the spring. Maybe Cornelius is a case in point. After a lifetime shoveling snow, and we can get as much as ten feet in a typical winter, they aim to take it easier when they retire."

"A pity," Mason said, resignedly, "that we cannot interview him. But at least we should take a look at Rollrock Ridge, now that we have come this far."

"I'll drive you up there right now," the American offered, "and let you have a look round while I make a routine call in Lincoln, just north of Waterville Valley."

That said, they piled back into the squad car and headed out along Route 104 to New Hampton, where they joined Interstate 93. Just under an hour later, after a scenic drive through the White Mountains, they left the highway and proceeded along a minor road until they came to a rustic sign announcing Rollrock Ridge. A dirt road through dense woodland led them to their destination. Captain Wells dropped them off at a parking lot full of trade vehicles, promising to return within the hour.

The Scotland Yard pair were surprised at what they found. Instead of a half-developed, abandoned site, they discovered a hive of activity. The hotel, as central feature, was nearing completion and crews were putting finishing touches to the chalets. Extensive gardens overlooking a small lake were being landscaped, turf was being laid and saplings planted. Glancing round for someone to speak with, they at length came across the site overseer as he was briefing an interior designer on décor for the hotel restaurant. The overseer, Henry Abbot, took them for prospective buyers.

"We aim to open by mid-summer," he informed them, jovially.

Any lingering suspicion George Mason might have harbored that he would discover Walter Cornelius at the site swiftly evaporated. His involvement seemed firmly in the past.

"Who are the current owners here?" he enquired, as the overseer was showing them the public areas of the hotel.

"Rollrock Ridge is owned by a consortium of bankers," Abbot explained.

Mason and Aubrey exchanged meaningful looks.

"I was looking for a Walter Cornelius," the detective said.

The overseer's face registered an ironic smile as he invited them to sit in the half-furnished lounge.

"Mr. Cornelius was the previous owner," he said. "I worked for him too, as site manager."

"Do you happen to know his present whereabouts?"

"Haven't heard from him in months," came the guarded reply. "But wait a minute. You're not interested in buying, are you? We still have unclaimed units."

"We are detectives, from Scotland Yard," Alison Aubrey explained, to his considerable astonishment, "investigating a murder case."

"You don't say so!" the other exclaimed. "When I heard your accent, I took you for prospective investors. We already have several British clients."

"Inspector George Mason, at your service," the detective announced. "And this is my colleague, Detective Sergeant Alison Aubrey."

"Pleased to meet you, I'm sure," the rather perplexed overseer said. "What can I do for you?"

"Can you possibly give me the names of the bankers in the consortium?" Mason then asked.

Henry Abbot regretfully shook his head.

"Can't help you there, I'm afraid. My briefings come directly from Alderney Mortgages."

"Then can you tell us what you know about Walter Cornelius?" Alison said.

"His luck was out," the other replied. "As I understand it, he invested a large part of his resources as deposit on this venture. The rest was to come from investors who bought residency rights in the form of chalets you no doubt noticed on your way in."

"And they couldn't afford to keep up payments in the economic downturn?" Alison asked, testing her pet theory.

"Several investors who had signed contracts simply backed out. Others, so I am told, lost well-paid jobs in the city. Mr. Cornelius was left high and dry. He couldn't meet the loan repayments and was foreclosed, after trying unsuccessfully to get extended bank credit."

"He lost most of his money?"

Henry Abbot nodded.

"My own view," he said, "for what it is worth, is that he overpaid in the first place. The initial valuation to fix the loan amount was high, in anticipation of a continuing boom in the property market. Values seemed to be going up and up until, of course, they went into reverse."

"Did Alderney provide the initial valuation?" Mason asked.

"From what little I know about that side of the business," the overseer explained, "and it is rather little, since I handle the practical aspects of these projects, the normal procedure is for a different company to do the initial valuation. A loan company such as Alderney Mortgages would then have an independent appraisal to quote in the event of any dispute."

"Chapman & Wilks," the Scotland Yard pair said, in chorus.

"I beg your pardon?" asked a bemused Henry Abbot.

"It's the name of a real estate services company we both know of," George Mason explained, "based in the Channel Islands."

"Mr. Cornelius has not come to any harm, I trust?" the other then asked, with evident concern.

"Not in so far as we know," Alison Aubrey replied. "We have never met him, in fact. As things are just now, we may not do so. His property at Meredith seems to have remained unoccupied for quite some time, although he still pays local taxes on it."

"He does travel quite a lot, I do know that. He also, I believe, spent some time in Hollywood, earlier in his career."

"As a film actor?" Alison asked, her eyes widening.

"Character roles were his specialty, I believe," Abbot rather vaguely replied. "I am not aware that he ever played a leading man. On the other hand, I don't watch movies all that much. I prefer a good book. But the rumor is that cinema is where he made most of his money."

At that point, the interior designer approached the overseer about a problem in the restaurant. Henry Abbot rose to excuse himself.

"Mustn't get behind schedule," he said. "You are very welcome to take a good look round the grounds, at your leisure. One day, you might even be interested in buying."

"On a policeman's salary?" George Mason asked, with heavy irony.

"You could always win the lottery, George," his young colleague quipped.

*

"A worthwhile trip, wouldn't you say?" George Mason remarked to Alison, as they sat down to dinner later that day at the indoor lakeside restaurant Captain Wells had recommended.

"An eye-opener, for sure," she agreed, "in more ways than one. Did you know that Rollrock Ridge is just inside White Mountains National Park? I had no idea it would be such stunning scenery."

"What amazed me was the advanced state of the project. They are expecting their first occupants in July already."

"The new management are certainly not dragging their feet," Alison remarked, as they scanned the menu.

Captain Wells had advised them to arrive early, saying that the restaurant was very popular and would fill up by seven o'clock. They had taken his tip and were rewarded with a window table for two overlooking the broad expanse of water tinted a reddish-gold by the setting sun. Mason was pleased with the choice of venue, as he watched a lone yacht tack into the wind on its return to the marina on the far side of the bay.

"What's your fancy?" he asked his companion, as the waitress hovered nearby.

"I'm going to start with clam chowder," Alison decided. "I understand it's a typical New England dish. For entrée, I think I'll have steak au poivre."

"I'll join you with the chowder," Mason said, "but I'll follow with the grilled lake-trout."

"And to drink?" the waitress politely enquired.

He quickly scanned the wine list.

"A bottle of Malbec, I should think."

The girl departed with their order and they watched the nearby tables fill up with family groups. What struck Alison was their casual dress, compared to patrons of establishments of similar standing in England, where jacket and tie would be mandatory. She remarked as much to her colleague.

"They don't stand much on ceremony in New Hampshire," he agreed. "There's a decidedly rustic feel about this whole area to me, which frankly I quite like. None of the stuffiness and conventions of city life."

"You're a countryman at heart, aren't you, George?" she remarked.

"I certainly could be, given half a chance. When I retire, a place like The Old Manse up in Buttermere would suit me just fine."

His companion fell silent for a while, concentrating on her soup. Pausing momentarily, she said:

"How do you rate Paul Richardson as a suspect, in view of what we've learned here?"

"It's a toss-up between the two," he replied, sampling his wine. "Richardson was in Amsterdam at the time of the incident. He also has access to weaponry and a strong-enough motive. The trouble is, we're not going to get much out of him while he remains behind bars."

"So the evidence against him remains circumstantial?"

George Mason nodded, dipping the last of his bread roll into his chowder before nudging the bowl aside.

"As it is with Walter Cornelius, at this point," he said. "Another elusive quarry. What intrigues me is that bit of information Henry Abbot slipped to us, that Rollrock Ridge is currently owned by a consortium of bankers."

"Are you thinking what I am thinking?" Alison asked him.

"That Conrad Fields and Willem de Vries are named as members of that consortium? It's certainly worth looking into, Alison. Since we have to return to London tomorrow, we'll ask Captain Wells to check the New Hampshire registry of companies, which may possibly list the two bankers as partners. He can fax anything he digs up to us later at Scotland Yard."

"Is he still joining us at our hotel for breakfast?"

"If nothing unforeseen turns up," George Mason said. "He lives quite close by, at a place called Sanbornton, I think he said. He'll meet us at eight o'clock on his way to Littleton, which is a fair drive north from Rollrock Ridge, on Interstate 93."

"An uneasy thought just struck me," Alison then said, tackling her peppered steak.

"And what is that, Alison?"

"There will presumably be other bankers in that consortium, besides Fields and de Vries. What if their lives are also at risk?"

George Mason laid down his fork and stopped eating for a few moments. He gazed beyond the window, as dusk descended over the tranquil water, raised his glass and took a thoughtful sip of the robust wine.

"That's a very interesting point, Alison," he said, eventually. "But, on the other hand, there hasn't been an attempt on a bank manager's life since March. It is now early May."

"Hardly more than a month," his young colleague remarked.

"Has it occurred to you that the two previous attacks were carried out on a Friday, exactly two weeks apart, on March 17 and March 31, respectively?"

Alison averted her gaze and glanced downwards, smilingly shaking her head while absorbed in her meal. Her companion, a little bemused at her reaction, resumed his interest in lake food. He formed the distinct impression that she wasn't taking his last remark very seriously.

"Are you into numerology now, George?" she asked, barely suppressing a smile.

The senior detective nearly choked on his food at the unexpected remark. Grasping his glass of iced water, he took a quick gulp and said:

"I am merely trying to establish a pattern, by your leave. I assure you, Sergeant Aubrey, that I have no truck with numerology, astrology or even alchemy, for that matter. In fact, I caused a stir at the Yard some years back by refusing the services of a famous clairvoyant. It was a missing person case. Bill Harrington will fill you in on that."

Alison gazed sympathetically back at her colleague. Sensing that she had ruffled his feathers a little, she raised her glass:

"Here's to your next big success," she proposed.

George Mason clinked his glass with hers and returned a wry smile.

"We'll await developments," he said, pensively. "I have the feeling a lot is yet to surface in this investigation. Even on a brief trip like this, we have gathered useful information."

"Show me the photograph of Walter Cornelius that Captain Wells gave you," she requested.

Mason drew out the original sales brochure printed for Rollrock Ridge. It featured a photograph of a smiling, upbeat individual in early middle age."

"Lucky for us Wells came across it," Alison said. "Cornelius is rather good-looking, isn't he? And, do you know, he reminds me of someone."

"You've seen him before?" her surprised senior enquired.

"Yes, but I can't place precisely where. You say that Captain Wells retrieved it from a local realtor's?"

Mason nodded.

"They had an outdated stack of the original brochures in a filing cabinet. Hadn't got round to discarding them."

"So at least we have a good idea of how he looks, even if we don't know where he is."

"We'll keep it on file back at the Yard," Mason said. "I'm sure it will prove useful. Now, what's for afters?"

"Blueberry cheesecake looks good to me," the young woman replied, scanning the dessert menu. "New England, and Maine especially, is noted for wild blueberries."

"I'll make do with a coffee," her senior said, as usual concerned about his waistline.

After their meal, since trade had eased off and there was no pressure to vacate their table, the two detectives relaxed with coffee and liqueurs, as dusk descended over the lake beyond the picture windows of the restaurant. Conversation took a more personal turn.

"Any young men in your life?" he asked, with an almost paternal air.

His companion flushed slightly at the directness of the question. Was the Inspector getting his own back for her earlier remark about numerology, she wondered?

"There have been one or two," she replied, as evenly as she could. "But nothing serious, as yet. I'm really just finding my feet after my transfer to London."

"That reminds me, Alison. I must give Adele a ring before we leave tomorrow. It'll be too late, past midnight in the UK, when we get back to the hotel."

"I've never met your wife," Alison said.

"That will happen all in good time. You must come to one of our barbecues when the summer finally arrives. Adele is a marvelous cook."

"I should very much like that. Where did you two meet?" she asked, her curiosity piqued.

"Believe it or not, we met on a skiing holiday in northern Italy."

"It can't get much more romantic than that!"

"Apres-ski," George Mason explained. "Both our tour groups were staying in the same hotel, operated by Club Mediterranee. They organized dances in the evenings after dinner. By the end of the week, I had gotten to know her quite well, and we agreed to meet up again on our return to London."

"I bet you're quite a good skier, too." Alison remarked.

"I think I could be," her companion hedged, "if only I could get to the slopes more often. Tried it in the Scottish Cairngorms once, but it was too icy. I fell all over the place."

"Which is probably why most people go to Europe," she said.

"You bet, Alison. Now, let me settle this bill and we'll stroll back to our hotel and catch up on some sleep."

CHAPTER SEVEN

Milovan Piric arrived in Copenhagen towards the end of the first week in May. Having reached Bremen safely following his flight from Amsterdam, he had lodged overnight in a sailors' hostel on the waterfront, proceeding to Hamburg the next day. He had holed up there for a few days, in the comparative safety of a large, anonymous city, hoping to meet again the man he knew only as Jason. The latter, however, had already left for the Danish capital, informing him of the fact poste restante at Hamburg's main post office. Aware that his hired gun would pass through the German port en route to Scandinavia, they had pre-arranged use of Hamburg's main post office for what in spy circles would be called a dead-letter drop. The letter instructed Piric to report to the Little Mermaid Cafe on Copenhagen's Inner Harbor at around 4 p.m.

He had left the Hauptbahnhof by the mid-morning service via Lubeck, arriving in the Danish capital just before three o'clock. As he walked past Tivoli Gardens, he reflected on his narrow escape from the Dutch police. If it hadn't been for Queen Day throughout Holland, he felt sure he would have been apprehended. More disturbingly, the officer on duty outside the bank manager's hospital room had recognized him instantly, which could only mean that Interpol had re-circulated his likeness, probably from a military photograph, to police forces within the European Union. That unforeseen setback had prompted him to take steps to alter his appearance. His beard was coming on nicely, he considered; and he had also visited a hairdresser's in Hamburg to have his thinning hair dyed a lighter color. A pair of dark glasses, along with the adoption of a seaman's attire, completed his disguise. As he cleared the famous gardens and turned into Vester Voldgade, which led directly down to Inner Harbor, he felt confident that no Danish police officer would give him a second glance.

Jason was finishing a snack of pickled herrings as he entered the run-down cafe. He glanced up with that rather wry, disapproving look of his.

"Hardly recognized you," he said, after a few moments. "Glad you could make it on time."

"I left Hamburg on the 10.37 a.m. express," Milovan Piric informed him, taking a seat and ordering hot tea with a shot of whiskey.

"By the way, great disguise you've adopted. Is this some sort of practical joke?"

Now came the hard part for the Serb: to explain to his temporary employer exactly what had gone wrong in Amsterdam. He swallowed hard and recounted the events of that fateful evening.

"So you needed to adjust your appearance?" Jason eventually asked, taking some time to absorb the unwelcome news. "Good thinking on your part. You look for all the world like you just stepped off a tramp steamer."

"I should think my disguise is fairly foolproof."

"Which is more than can be said of your professional skills, Milovan," the other was quick to retort.

The Serb glanced downwards, shifting his feet nervously.

"I must admit," Jason continued, "that when I hired you, I was not aware that you had a criminal record. It rather complicates matters."

"It's a chance you take if you hire a professional hit-man," Piric replied, in his own defense. "We are hardly going to be squeaky-clean, are we?"

Jason pushed the remains of his dish aside, sat back and observed his hire closely, as if weighing the odds. Eventually, a faint smile spread across his taut features.

"The game is still on," he said. "I hired you for the whole nine yards and you will be paid in full at the end of the contract, minus the advance you received at Hoorn."

Milovan Piric felt a keen sense of relief. He sipped his spiked tea made, he noted, with East African leaf, and waited for the other man to return from a visit to the men's room, wondering about him. He knew nothing at all of Jason's background, or how he came to be in one

European city after another. Was he some kind of salesman, or perhaps in the travel business? And what precisely was his motive in all this?

"What happened in Amsterdam was regrettable," Jason said, on regaining his seat. "An unfortunate lapse, in fact. On the other hand, Willem de Vries may not recover consciousness. Latest update, according to the newspapers, is that he remains in a coma. I personally doubt he will recover."

"You are saying I should proceed to Stockholm, as planned?" the Serb asked, his confidence returning.

"By all means," the other replied. "When you arrive in the Swedish capital, you are to make your way to Hotel Malmo, in Gamla Stan, the oldest part of the city. Accommodation has been reserved for you on the evening of May 11. On the following day, immediately after the event, you are to proceed by taxi to the coastal town of Kapellskar, where you will take the ferry to Marienhamn in the Oland Islands, half-way between Sweden and Finland. You will rest up there until you receive further instructions from me, by letter addressed to your hotel."

"The hotel being...?" Piric asked, impressed at the other's detailed planning.

"The Cecilie. It's named after a famous tea-clipper out of Marienhamn, the Herzogin Cecilie."

"On the lines of the Cutty Sark?" the other asked.

"You've got it. They were the fastest full-riggers afloat, round the Cape of Good Hope to India, before the age of steam."

*

"There has been a development," Bill Harrington informed George Mason at the start of their morning conference, the day following the latter's return from New England.

The mildly jet-lagged detective waited for his senior to elaborate.

"The gunman paid a return visit to Royal Hospital, Amsterdam, in a bid to finish the job. Luckily for de Vries, the man was recognized by the duty officer stationed outside the private ward. He gave chase, but the assailant disappeared in a crowd of revelers celebrating – would you believe it? – Queen Day."

"How did the Dutch policeman recognize him?" an intrigued George Mason wanted to know.

The Chief Inspector drew from his desk drawer the Interpol circular and passed it across to his colleague, who examined it with evident puzzlement.

"Something the matter, Inspector?" Harrington asked.

"It's not the same person," an incredulous George Mason said, in turn drawing the Rollrock Ridge brochure from his jacket and passing it across the desk.

Bill Harrington then compared the two likenesses.

"You're right there, old chap," he said. "Is the Walter Cornelius shown here in this brochure meant to be a suspect? If so, you're barking up the wrong tree. He doesn't bear the slightest resemblance to the gunman, whom Interpol have on record for a crime committed two years ago in Hungary. He's been on the run since then. His name is Milovan Piric, a former non-commissioned officer in the Serbian Army."

George Mason sat back and scratched his head. This was a totally unexpected turn-up, after what he had considered a promising expedition across the Atlantic. Could he be on the wrong track altogether, he wondered?

"The department has run to considerable expense at a difficult time," Harrington irritably continued, "to send the pair of you to New Hampshire, without anything more to show for it than a case of mistaken identity."

Mason winced inwardly. He felt sure he was on to something useful, but he would have a hard time convincing his superior.

"I'm wondering, Inspector," Harrington then said, "if I should keep you on this case, since there are so many other pressing matters to attend to. Why not let the Dutch authorities handle it? It's on their watch, after all."

"Because one of murders took place right here in London," George Mason countered. "I think we have an obligation to stay with this case, until justice is fully served."

Harrington took his time before answering, allowing that his colleague had a valid point.

"In view of your previous record," he said, eventually. "I'll give you a little more time to come up with something more concrete. I allow that your methods are a little unconventional, but you've proved your worth on more than one occasion."

"That is very generous of you, Chief Inspector. I'll do my utmost to justify your confidence."

Back in his own office, Mason sat at his desk and weighed his superior's words carefully. More than likely, he thought, the Superintendent was breathing down Harrington's neck and pressing for results. At the same time, he had to admit to himself that this Milovan Piric, whoever he was, had now emerged as a significant player in the game, surfacing out of nowhere. He drew out the half-profile Identi-kit picture of the assailant taken at National Indemnity's premises in the City and compared it with the full-face Interpol circular. It seemed quite possible, but not absolutely certain, that they depicted the same person.

At that point, Detective Sergeant Aubrey put her head round the door.

"Not intruding, am I, George?" she enquired.

"By no means, Alison. Step right in."

"This fax from Concord, New Hampshire just came through to the general office," she said, handing it to him.

George Mason took it and quickly scanned the contents.

"This gives us the names and professional status of the current owners of Rollrock Ridge," he announced.

"And, interestingly enough," Alison added, "they are all bankers."

"An international consortium, too, by the look of it. The New Hampshire state registry has not yet been amended to show the demise of Conrad Fields. That, no doubt, will take time, bureaucracy being what it is. But we also have here a Stig Lagerqvist, manager of Vardagsbank, Stockholm and an Urpo Koivonen, who runs Karelia Pankki in Helsinki."

"Do you think their lives may be in danger, too?" a concerned Alison asked.

"Hard to say at this point. The Amsterdam hit, and probably the London one too, was apparently done by a Serb named Milovan Piric, about whom we know very little beyond the fact that he has a prior record. Since there hasn't been a similar attack in almost a month, we may be in the clear. Bill Harrington has half a mind to leave matters with the Dutch authorities."

"Surely you persuaded him otherwise," Alison remonstrated, "after all the groundwork we've put in?"

"He's prepared to let it ride for the time being, but we must come up with something more concrete soon. This fax may, or may not, provide the key."

"What do you propose to do about these additional names?"

"I'll get Donald Dinwiddie, our forensic accountant, to check them out. He is more experienced in corporate affairs than I am."

He picked up the desk phone and placed an internal call.

"Donald," he said, "I'd like you to go over to Companies House in the Strand and see what you can dig up about a Stig Lagerqvist and an Urpo Koivonen. They're registered in New Hampshire as co-owners of Rollrock Ridge, along with Conrad Fields and Willem de Vries. I particularly need to know if they also have business connections here in the UK."

"Company directorships, you mean?" Dinwiddie asked him.

"Anything along those lines," George Mason said, "including major shareholdings or interests in British firms."

"Will this afternoon be soon enough? I'm a bit tied-up just now trying to trace some dud checks passed at the recent Earls Court small arms exhibition."

"If you can fit it in today, Donald, that will be very helpful. Harrington's breathing down my neck."

"Get him a bottle of Glenfiddich," Dinwiddie roguishly suggested. "That should mollify him."

Alison Aubrey returned to the general office to resume routine duties. Hardly had George Mason put the phone down and begun sorting through his correspondence than he received a call from the Chief Inspector.

Speak of the devil, he mused.

"Inspector Mason," Bill Harrington said, "I want you to go directly to the interview room, where a Mr. Paul Richardson is waiting to speak with you."

"How the Dickens...?" the surprised detective began, but Harrington had already rung off.

What a turn-up, he considered, as he made his way down a long corridor to a room at the far end, where a uniformed constable stood on duty by the door. He entered to find the wiry, athletic ex-S.A.S. officer seated behind the bare table with a staff technician preparing to make a recording. Two metal chairs and an overhead lamp completed the sparse furnishings.

"Paul Richardson?" Mason asked.

"The same," came the curt reply. He started to rise, but the detective motioned him to remain seated.

"I must confess," George Mason then said, taking the chair opposite him, "to being more than a little surprised at your sudden re-surfacing."

Richardson essayed a thin smile.

"My wife mentioned when I rang her that you wished to meet me on my way through London. I understand you were in my neck of the woods a short time ago, where Anne received you."

The detective nodded.

"But aren't you supposed to be in custody in the North African Republic?" he asked.

Richardson's smile broadened.

"I was released yesterday," he said, "through the good offices of our man in M'bala, the British Consul. Not before time, either, given the appalling conditions."

"You were not, then, implicated in the abortive coup?"

The ex-S.A.S. man shook his head vigorously.

"I was duped by the Defense Minister, Patrick Nokubia, into supplying machine pistols for the presidential bodyguard. Instead, they were issued to Nokubia's backers, a group of disaffected senior officers. After a skirmish lasting all of twelve hours, forces loyal to the president overpowered them. The ringleaders are now in jail awaiting trial."

"Machine pistols?" Mason enquired. "You mean automatic weapons that can be loaded with a magazine?"

Richardson nodded.

"Quite lethal, I am sure. And this hardware was supplied by…?"

"Mueller & Wolf, a German firm based in Wurzburg and Kassel ."

"Whom you contacted in Amsterdam on March 31 last?"

Richardson returned a look of considerable surprise, wondering how the person opposite him could be so well-informed about his doings.

Certainly, Anne could have told him nothing, since she knew little of his business affairs.

"That is correct," he grudgingly acknowledged.

"Where exactly were you on the morning of that day, March 31, between the hours of eight and nine in the morning?"

Richardson thought for a moment and said:

"I left my hotel at around 8.15 a.m., soon after taking breakfast. As it was a fine day, I made my way on foot to the consulate of the North African Republic."

"Can anyone corroborate your movements?"

The ex-S.A.S. man shook his head, returning for the first time a rather anxious look.

"Did you speak with anyone on the way?"

"No, I did not."

"What impressions did you form of the Dutch capital on that morning?" Mason then asked.

"I recall that they were erecting wooden stalls," the other replied, "for what seemed to me to be an outsize street-market. London's Petticoat Lane on a grand scale, you might say. Oh, and they were putting up orange bunting and flags."

"Did you happen to know the reason?"

"Ludwig Koch, my contact from Germany, mentioned something about a national day, on the lines of Bastille Day in France."

"A bit less republican," George Mason wryly commented. "They were making early preparations for Queen Day, which the Dutch observe every spring."

Paul Richardson exchanged the briefest of smiles with the recording technician at his interviewer's dry sense of humor.

"Perhaps we could institute something on those lines in Britain," he remarked. "A national holiday to mark Her Majesty's birthday in June."

"Did you go directly from your hotel to the consulate?" Mason then asked, ignoring the remark.

"Apart from a spot of shopping on the way, yes I did. I stopped to buy perfume for Anne and some Dutch cigars for myself."

"How well did you know Willem de Vries?"

"I did not know him personally," the other replied, evidently surprised at the question. "But I knew of him. I believe he was a director of Alderney Mortgages. He was named as such on their letterhead."

"What was your reaction when they foreclosed on your Lake District development?"

"I was furious as all hell," the other replied. "If they had given me a little more time, say, into the summer months, I think the project might well have succeeded. I sank a great deal of money into it."

"Did you harbor any ill will towards your lender on that account?"

"I certainly didn't regard them as my fairy godmother," came the tart reply.

The detective made brief notes, glancing occasionally at his interlocutor to see if his facial expression belied his words.

"Were you aware that de Vries has been shot?" he asked, after a while. "And that he now lies in a coma at Royal Hospital, Amsterdam?"

"Anne mentioned something about that when I spoke with her last evening. Is he going to pull through?"

"Touch-and-go, at the present," Mason replied, intrigued that a potential suspect should enquire about a victim's health. It could be an artful subterfuge.

"I sincerely hope he recovers."

"How well do you know Milovan Piric?" the detective then asked.

"I know no one of that name."

"Didn't you, as a member of Special Air Services, serve with NATO forces in Bosnia in the spring of 1994?"

"I certainly did, but mainly in a peace-keeping role between the Serbs and the Kosovars."

"So you would have had the opportunity to meet with combatants on both sides?"

"I certainly made contacts, but only in the line of military duty."

"Then it is quite possible that you met with Milovan Piric, a non-commissioned officer in the Serb Army?"

"I think, Inspector," Richardson then said, "that I should like my lawyer to be present before we take this matter any further."

"This is merely a preliminary interview, Mr. Richardson," George Mason assured him. "We are not at this stage making any charges. You are quite free to leave this building, which you entered of your own free will, and return to Buttermere, where I am sure your wife Anne will be highly relieved to greet you."

The ex-S.A.S. man rose to leave.

"Please remain seated," the detective said, "until I formally close the interview."

"I am at your disposal," the other tersely replied.

"What are your tastes in literature?"

Richardson's eyes opened wide at such an unexpected question.

"I don't read much fiction," he replied, "if that's what you are referring to."

"How about Somerset Maugham?"

"I read one or two of his novels, years ago. Can't recall their names."

"Both you and your wife belong to a book club, I understand."

"Is that a misdemeanor nowadays, Inspector?"

"Of course not," Mason replied. "A little unexpected, perhaps, for a person with your active background."

"We joined mainly to give Anne a social outlet. Life can be very quiet in the Lake District after the main tourist season. I accompany her on occasion, that's all; especially if there is a special event, like a visiting personality, a lecture on something topical, or a discussion about a well-known author."

"Such as Wallace Stevens?"

"His name came up quite recently," the other replied, with a neutral expression.

"Do the words Money is a kind of poetry mean anything to you?"

Mason watched the man closely for sign of any reaction, but Richardson merely seemed intrigued, taking his time to weigh the thought-provoking statement. Eventually, he said:

"Gorgonzola cheese could be a kind of poetry, for that matter. It depends entirely on how you look at things. Ballet, for example, is sometimes referred to as poetry in motion."

George Mason smiled to himself. The man was no fool if he could come up at short notice with an observation like that.

"You are free to go now, Mr. Richardson," he suddenly said. "I appreciate that you came forward voluntarily, of your own accord. I shall contact you again in the near future, pending further investigations. Give my regards to your wife Anne and thank her on my behalf for her co-operation and assistance."

"I shall remain at Buttermere for the immediate future," Richardson said, rising to his feet with a rather world-weary expression. "Had my fill of foreign parts for a while."

When the ex-S.A.S. officer had left the building, Mason returned to his desk deep in thought. It was a long shot, perhaps, trying to tie Paul Richardson in with Milovan Piric, who had been identified as the gunman. Both men had military backgrounds and were experienced in weaponry. And it was at least possible that they had previously met in Serbia. They were also both in Amsterdam on that fateful morning. But were they in cahoots? He would give a lot to know the answer to that question. All that he now knew for certain was that neither Paul Richardson nor Walter Cornelius had pulled the trigger.

CHAPTER EIGHT

The following morning, George Mason scheduled an early meeting with the forensic accountant, Donald Dinwiddie. The canny Scot had completed his researches at Companies House in the Strand the previous afternoon; while Mason, after his interview with Paul Richardson, had gone down to Dulwich to tie up some loose ends regarding a break-in at the college library. Some rare books and illuminated manuscripts had been taken but, oddly enough, the valuable collection of paintings had been left untouched.

"Was your trip fruitful?" the detective enquired, as the Scot sat facing him across the cluttered desk.

Dinwiddie gave a curt nod, drawing a file from his briefcase.

"Stig Lagerqvist has several business interests in Britain," he said. "He is part-owner of a firm based in Newcastle that operates ski-touring holidays in Norway. He is also a non-executive director of National Indemnity."

"You don't say so!" Mason exclaimed. "That could be highly significant. Did you turn up anything else?"

"He's also a director of a real estate services company in Jersey."

"Don't tell me the name. I'll hazard a guess."

The Scot glanced up from his notes, expectantly.

"Chapman & Wilks," the detective announced, with evident satisfaction.

"Right first time," the other said, impressed. "Interestingly enough, Urpo Koivonen is also on the board of Chapman & Wilks. For a relatively small services company, with capitalization of under a quarter of a million pounds, they appear to have an international reach."

George Mason leaned back in his swivel chair and pondered the implications.

"You know, Donald, that strikes me as rather curious. Conrad Fields, Willem de Vries, Stig Lagerqvist and Urpo Koivonen are also registered in Concord, New Hampshire, as members of the consortium that now owns Rollrock Ridge."

"The resort you mentioned in the White Mountains?"

The detective nodded.

"But how do Chapman & Wilks fit into the picture?"

"They're the people who did the initial valuation of the project, before Alderney Mortgages approved the loan. I established that much during my earlier visit to Jersey."

The Scot sat bolt upright and fixed him with a thoughtful look. He then began quietly drumming with his finger-tips on the desk top, as if in time with his thought process.

"What you are telling me, George," he said, after deliberating for a while, "is that two of the bankers in the new ownership consortium were directors of Alderney Mortgages; while the other two, the Swede and the Finn, were on the board of Chapman & Wilks."

"Doesn't the law require an independent property valuation before a mortgage loan is granted?" Mason asked.

"In this country, it certainly does. But I'm not so sure about the Channel Islands. A real estate services company based off-shore, say in Jersey or the Cayman Islands, would not necessarily be subject to British law."

"They could set any value they liked on a given property?" a surprised George Mason asked.

"In theory, yes," Dinwiddie conceded. "There is, in fact, a somewhat similar case before the High Court at the present time. I've been following it closely. The plaintiff is claiming collusion between a leading bank and a supposedly independent valuer to inflate the price of a property before the loan was granted. And, furthermore – this is the interesting bit – they did it fully anticipating that the borrower might be unable to meet the loan repayments in an economic downturn if, for example, he lost his job."

"So that the lenders could foreclose and seize the assets for themselves?"

"That is precisely the brunt of the High Court case I just mentioned."

Mason's face registered genuine astonishment. He weighed the Scot's words carefully and said:

"So this situation I've been investigating at Rollrock Ridge could have been deliberately engineered by Alderney Mortgages in cahoots with Chapman & Wilks, to take advantage of the developer, Walter Cornelius?"

"I'm not saying that is the case," Dinwiddie cautiously replied. "Only that it may be so. It has happened before – witness the on-going High Court case."

"We may now have a clearer motive for crime," Mason suggested, rising to his feet and pacing the room.

"You mean that, rather than seek redress in court in the normal way, an aggrieved party has taken the law into his own hands and shot two of the bankers involved?"

"It's beginning to look that way to me, Donald. Cornelius, whereabouts unknown, and Richardson, just released from captivity, both have sufficient motive. But the fact that the banking consortium is now the effective owner of Rollrock Ridge inclines me to suspect the former. And what is more, two more lives may now be on the line."

"Stig Lagerqvist and Urpo Koivonen?" Dinwiddie prompted.

The detective nodded and resumed his seat.

"But the consortium may also now own The Derwent Club," the Scot continued. "Which would place both your suspects on a roughly equal footing, as far as motive is concerned."

"Go back to Companies House as soon as you can," Mason advised, "and establish if that is the case."

"Tomorrow morning would my earliest opportunity."

"Join me around noon at The Hop Pole on the Strand. It's just a few blocks from Companies House."

"I know it well," Dinwiddie said. "It's one of my favorite city pubs. They do an excellent plowman's lunch. And they have hand-pulled Scottish ale on tap."

"Cheddar cheese with pickles, whole grain bread? I'll go for that," the detective said. "My main reservation in this intriguing case, now that we have established a plausible motive, is that the previous incidents took place exactly two weeks apart, both of them on a Friday. Today is Friday, May 12, exactly four weeks later. There have been no further incidents."

"Then your theory may be wide of the mark," the forensic accountant remarked.

"Which would be good news for Lagerqvist and Koivonen, at the very least," Mason wryly responded.

*

Milovan Piric rose early on the morning of May 12, putting on the suit Jason had left for him in a parcel at Reception. He then went downstairs for a typical Swedish breakfast of rye porridge, followed by an open sandwich of hard-boiled egg with anchovies. With his coffee, he indulged in a Danish pastry. After eating and scanning the local newspaper, he returned to his room, brushed his teeth, combed his growing beard and fitted the silencer to his Ruger pistol, which he placed securely in his shoulder holster before checking out of Hotel Malmo shortly before eight o'clock. He then made his way through the narrow streets of Gamla Stan towards The Old Post Office, where he found Jason's letter waiting for him poste restante.

Finding a secluded spot in a small enclosure between medieval buildings, he sat down on a wooden bench and slit open the letter. It contained a rough street map showing the location of Vardagsbank, complete with a ground-floor plan showing the manager's office to the left of the reception area and the exact position of the emergency exit. He checked his watch: it was 8.16 a.m. The premises would open at precisely 8.30 a.m. Jason had pre-booked an appointment for him with the manager, Stig Lagerqvist, for 8.45 a.m., in the name of Brad Weston.

With a few minutes to kill, he lit a Dutch cigarillo and watched young mothers arrive with small children and drop them off at the kindergarten across the street. The youngsters gathered in a play area under trees, their bubbly, innocent chatter contrasting markedly with his own somber mood. He found, in the course of his brief introduction to it, that he quite liked Stockholm and could spend more time here. The Baltic Sea came right into the heart of the city, allowing liners to berth within a short walking distance of the main amenities. The air was clean and bracing, with a tang of salt. The natives, while not unfriendly, seemed more reserved than southern Europeans and inclined to mind their own business. It suited him that no one had paid him the least attention, not even in the hotel dining-room or in the comfortable lounge, where he had relaxed after his journey from Copenhagen.

After ten minutes, he rose from the bench and commenced walking past The Old Post Office to the second opening on the right, which he identified from the street sign as Birgergatan. Double-checking the rough sketch Jason had provided, he proceeded along it until he reached his objective. The old, four-storey building was situated on a corner facing the more modern premises of the Bank of Stockholm. Most pedestrian traffic seemed directed there, rather than to his objective, Vardagsbank, which Jason had informed him was a relatively small concern with branches confined to Stockholm and its hinterland. Stepping inside, he approached Reception, confident that his disguise made him unrecognizable from the portrait which had been circulating in newspapers and on television channels.

"May I assist you?" the receptionist asked.

"I have an appointment with the manager," he announced, "regarding a mortgage application."

"Your name?" the woman asked, checking the appointments diary.

"Brad Weston."

"For 8.45 a.m.? Mr. Lagerqvist will be expecting you. Turn right and it's the second door on the left." She then picked up the phone to notify the manager.

"Tack so mycket," he said, employing his best Swedish. "Many thanks."

The receptionist smiled and indicated the general direction with a sweep of her hand. The visitor proceeded down the short corridor away from the reception area and knocked on the glass-paneled door.

"Enter."

Milovan Piric opened the door and stepped inside. The manager half rose to greet him.

"Mr. Weston?" he genially enquired. "Please take a seat."

The Serb sat down facing him across the polished walnut desk.

"What type of mortgage would you be seeking," the manager asked, "residential or commercial?"

Piric smiled thinly, fished inside his jacket pocket and withdrew a small slip of paper, which he passed across the desk. Lagerqvist took it, appraised it for a while with a quizzical expression, and read aloud:

"Business is other people's money?"

Evidently expecting some kind of explanation, he looked hard at his visitor, also trying to decide if he was British or American. When nothing was forthcoming, he asked:

"Is this some kind of pleasantry, Mr. Weston?"

"In a manner of speaking," Piric cryptically replied.

"I do hope you haven't come here on some frivolous errand," the manager continued, "simply to waste my time."

"Far from it," Piric replied. "I am here in deadly earnest."

With that, he sprang to his feet, withdrew his Ruger pistol and aimed it directly at the manager's heart. The latter, in sudden panic, reached for the alarm button and barely failed to activate it before he slumped forward across his desk, still clutching the slip of paper. Confident that the shot had not been heard, the assassin calmly replaced the pistol in its holster, closed the office door quietly behind him and made for the emergency exit. In the street outside, he stepped into the taxi which had been booked for him at precisely 8.50 a.m. The driver, greeting someone in a dark suit, took him for a normal business client of the bank. They had not proceeded very far along the narrow, congested streets of Gamla Stan before they heard a loud siren. The Serb's heart sank, that an alarm had gone off so soon. He figured that someone, perhaps a secretary, had entered the manager's office shortly after he had left.

"Could be a hold-up," the taxi driver said.

"Or a fire-alarm," the assassin suggested.

"That's probably more like it," the driver said. "It does happen from time to time. Somebody smoking a cigarette, most likely, beneath one of those temperamental wall sensors."

"Modern technology," the Serb remarked, sitting back in his seat as the cab began to make headway through the traffic. In a few minutes, they were crossing the bridge linking the old quarter with the more modern parts of the city.

"Where to?" the driver asked.

"Lidingo," Piric curtly replied, quickly checking that he had enough Swedish kronor to pay the fare. "Drop me at the bus station there."

Jason had told him to head for this northern suburb and take the express service from there to Kapellskar, on the Baltic coast. It would be more anonymous than arriving at the ferry terminal by taxi, since he might be recognized by the taxi driver from news programs later in the day. He would not want the Swedish police to suspect that he had embarked on a ferry at Kapellskar, since ships from there went in only one direction, to the Oland Islands; and from there to Turku on the south-west coast of Finland. When this assignment was concluded, he mused, as the cab wound its way through the compact center of Stockholm, he would use the generous compensation to buy a small farm in East Africa and accept mercenary assignments in the fallow season. There was no future for him in Europe, he considered, except as a fugitive. Being constantly on the move, or lying low, to escape detection held no appeal whatsoever. He was a man who needed an active life, preferably in the open air. The plains of the Serengeti spread out before him, in his mind's eye, as he sat back for the duration of the trip.

*

"Pack your overnight bag," George Mason told Alison Aubrey later that day when she returned to Scotland Yard after a routine call to a women's shelter in Stepney, in connection with a case of spousal abuse.

"Just like that?" she asked, a bit taken aback.

"There's been another incident," Mason informed her. "The manager of Vardagsbank in Stockholm was shot dead this morning. We're to go over there straight away. I managed to book a flight out of Heathrow at 10.42 a.m. tomorrow. Be at the terminal by 8.30 a.m. at the latest."

"Do you think it may be the same gunman?" the young sergeant asked.

"We won't know that until we get there. According to the Swedish police, he doesn't fit the portrait circulated by Interpol. He was dressed like a businessman, for one thing."

"He could have altered his appearance following his identification in Amsterdam," Alison suggested. "In fact, it would be rather surprising if he hadn't."

"You have a point there," her colleague agreed. "The victim, Stig Lagerqvist, was also, in common with Fields and de Vries, a member of the consortium that owns Rollrock Ridge. Furthermore, he was a director of Chapman & Wilks, the firm that undertook the initial valuation before Alderney Mortgages granted the loan. Donald Dinwiddie thinks there may have been collusion between those two companies, to take advantage of the laxer property laws in the Channel Islands. He thinks they may have deliberately inflated the value of the White Mountains resort, to increase the likelihood of default, followed by foreclosure."

"If Paul Richardson had any suspicion that technique might have applied to The Derwent Club, one could understand his fury."

"He may indeed have suspected it," George Mason allowed, "but he would have lacked hard evidence. He would have assumed that Chapman & Wilks gave independent and impartial advice, which is what such companies are supposed to do."

The young sergeant eased herself into a chair, to absorb the Inspector's line of reasoning. Not in a month of Sundays, she felt, would she herself have come up with such a theory.

"It would take someone like Donald to figure that out," she drily remarked.

"That's what forensic accountants are for, after all," Mason said. "And Dinwiddie is at the top of his game."

"Bill Harrington once told me he graduated cum laude in logic and moral philosophy from Edinburgh University."

"He was also awarded the Institute of Applied Accountancy's gold medal," her colleague added. "But enough said. I'm leaving in a few minutes to make arrangements with Adele. And, by the way, do you have a problem leaving at such short notice?"

"I did have a dental appointment first thing tomorrow morning," she replied, "but it's not all that urgent and can easily be re-scheduled. Do you think I should take warm clothing?"

The detective smiled at what he took to be undue concern.

"I think you can assume, Alison, that the Swedish climate in mid-May will be rather similar to the British. Pack an extra sweater, if you like, in case the evenings are a bit chill."

*

Kommissar Gunnar Ahlgren of the Stockholm Police was waiting to greet the Scotland Yard pair when they arrived around noon at Arlanda airport. He briefed them on the known details of the case during the twenty-mile drive through the province of Uppland to the Swedish capital.

"We know that the killer entered the premises of Vardagsbank shortly after opening time," the Kommissar said. "He checked in with the receptionist, who directed him to the manager's office."

"Then he must have pre-booked an appointment," George Mason said.

"In the name of Brad Weston. Ostensibly, it was in connection with a mortgage loan."

"That sounds appropriate," Alison Aubrey remarked.

"The receptionist, Liv Blofield, did not hear the shot," Ahlgren explained. "Nor did she notice the intruder pass her desk on his way out. So we are assuming that he left by the emergency exit, which is situated to the rear of the building behind the manager's office. It's possible that a vehicle was waiting for him, to assist his getaway. The bank premises were probably closely vetted beforehand."

Within fifty minutes, they had arrived in Gamla Stan. Since parking was restricted in the narrow street, Kommissar Ahlgren pulled the squad car partly onto the sidewalk and led the way inside. Liv Blofield stepped forward to greet them.

"This is Inspector Mason from Scotland Yard," the Kommissar said, quickly effecting introductions, "and his assistant, Detective Sergeant Aubrey."

"A dreadful business, Inspector," the receptionist said. "Mr. Lagerqvist was such a popular employer. Everybody loved and respected him."

"Can you give them a description of the intruder?" the Swedish officer then asked.

"He was about as tall as you are, Inspector," she replied. "With blond hair, which I think he colored, because his beard was a little darker. He was wearing a dark-blue business suit and lightly-shaded glasses. He said had come about a mortgage application. Mr. Lagerqvist was expecting him."

"Was it the same person who initially booked the appointment?" Alison asked.

"Impossible to say, really," the woman replied. "It was booked about a month ago, and we get a fair number of calls every day through my desk."

George Mason then showed her the Interpol portrait.

"Would you say that this was the same person?" he asked.

Liv Blofield examined the photo carefully and slowly shook her head.

"This is a younger man," she replied. "I do not see a strong resemblance."

"Did he speak English?" Alison asked.

"Yes, but with an accent. I have visited England several times and I am fairly familiar with regional accents. I would say he was almost certainly not a native of Britain, but could have been an immigrant."

"But definitely not American?" her colleague asked.

The receptionist nodded, emphatically.

"German was my first impression," she said. "Or possibly East European."

"Milovan Piric," Mason said, half aloud.

. "Could we take a look at the crime scene?" the Kommissar asked.

Liv Blofield led the way across the carpeted hall to the manager's office.

"Nothing has been touched," she said. "Only the forensic people from the Police Department have entered."

George Mason immediately noticed a crumpled slip of paper lying on the desk blotter.

"May I?" he enquired.

"Help yourself, Inspector," the Swede said.

Mason picked it up and read aloud: Business is other people's money.

Gunnar Ahlgren noted Alison Aubrey's immediate reaction, almost a Eureka moment.

"Do those words mean something to you?" he asked.

"They mean," George Mason informed him, "that we are dealing with the very same person who shot Conrad Fields, manager of National Indemnity in London. He also attacked Willem de Vries, of Zuider Bank in Amsterdam, who to this day has remained in a coma. Quotations like this, always about money, are his calling card. He has left one at each scene so far."

"You amaze me, Inspector," the Swede said, scratching his head. "Looks like he's taunting the victim, or the police, or both in some weird way."

"You can say that again!" Mason exclaimed, with feeling.

"Do you happen to know his identity?" the Kommissar then asked.

"Most probably, in fact I'm pretty certain, it is Milovan Piric, a former non-commissioned officer in the Serbian Army, as shown here on this Interpol circular. He was recognized by the police officer on duty at Royal Hospital, Amsterdam. It is evident from your receptionist's lack of recognition that he has since adopted a disguise. He would also be older by several years."

"So we put out an alert for a blond, bearded man wearing a dark-blue business suit?"

"He could be anywhere by now," Alison said, "over twenty-four hours later."

"Or he could be lying low here in Stockholm, waiting for the initial furor to die down."

"Do you have any idea where he stayed?" Mason asked.

"We checked the name Brad Weston with the city hotels," Gunnar Ahlgren explained, "on the assumption that he stayed overnight in order to be on the scene early the next day. Our hunch was correct. He did in fact spend the night of May 11 at Hotel Malmo, right here in Gamla Stan. We could call there now, if you think it may be helpful."

The Scotland Yard pair indicated their willingness. Thanking the receptionist for her assistance, they piled back into the squad car and held on tight as the Kommissar reversed sharply up the narrow street and took a right-hand turn, stopping minutes later outside Hotel Malmo. On entering the premises, they asked the duty clerk if they could see the room a Mr. Brad Weston had recently occupied.

The clerk checked the hotel register and gave the key to Room 41 to Gunnar Ahlgren, who led the way up flights of bare wooden steps to the fourth floor. Inserting the key in the lock, he opened the door and ushered the visitors inside. The room was neat as a new pin. The chambermaids had been in to remake the bed, vacuum the floor and place fresh spring flowers on the bedside table. George Mason first checked the waste-paper bin, but that too had been emptied.

"I don't expect we'll find much here," the Kommissar said, "not after the cleaners have done such a thorough job."

"Wait a minute," Alison Aubrey said, reaching into the top shelf of the wardrobe and pulling out a loosely-folded jacket and a pair of trousers, which she laid on the bed.

"Check the jacket pockets," Gunnar Ahlgren urged.

Alison immediately did so, drawing out some scraps of torn paper.

"What's this?" George Mason asked.

"Looks like a note that's been hastily torn up," Alison said, laying out the pieces on the dressing table.

"The Old …," Mason read, peering over her shoulder.

"That could be The Old Post Office," the Swede said, "a well-known landmark in Gamla Stan. And there seems to be part of a signature, too: Ja___; or possibly Jo___."

"Could mean a number of things," George Mason thought aloud. "If it's a person's name, it could be James, Jake, John, Joseph. Take your pick. It doesn't tell us a great deal."

"It may tell us quite a lot," Alison countered. "For one thing, if this note was addressed to Brad Weston, aka Milovan Piric, it could mean that he was directed to The Old Post Office by some other party."

"Where there could have been instructions waiting for him," the Kommissar added.

"That could be highly significant," Mason considered, after a moment's reflection. "If another party is involved, that might have some bearing on the cryptic quotations, which don't somehow fit an ex-army type like Piric."

"Suppose those letters refer to a Janice, a Jacqueline or a Joanne," Alison Aubrey countered. "The note could then refer to a romantic tryst."

"At a post office, Sergeant?" the incredulous Swede exclaimed. "Wouldn't a hotel be more likely?"

The young woman flushed slightly, but was undeterred.

"A message left poste restante could very well set up a rendezvous at a hotel," she argued.

"Either way," a judicious George Mason concluded, "we now have a new and possibly useful clue to the puzzle."

"I'll take these garments over to the lab," the Swede said. "They may contain traces of body fluids for DNA purposes."

"You'll have your work cut out to catch him, Kommissar," Mason said. "He's eluded the authorities in at least three countries so far."

"If he's still in Sweden, we'll make it our business to track him down. We have an advantage over London and Amsterdam in that our cities are not very large. Strangers stand out more easily from the crowd."

Gunnar Ahlgren then glanced at his watch.

"Must be getting back to H.Q," he said. "I still have your suitcases in the trunk. I'll drop you by your hotel on my way."

"Hotel Djurgaard," Mason informed him.

"I know it. It's right by the zoo."

"I expect we shall see some portions of your fascinating city, while we have the opportunity," Mason said. "What do you say, Detective Sergeant?"

"If I can rest awhile and freshen up first," she agreed, the hectic start to the day having caught up with her.

"I'd willingly have been your guide," the Swede said, "but there is an important Rotary meeting tonight for choosing the new president. Can't skip it."

On their way past Reception, George Mason checked with the duty clerk that a package had been left for a Mr. Brad Weston two days ago. He referred to it when, two hours later, the Scotland Yard pair were dining at a small. homely restaurant off the main shopping center.

"The clothes you found in the wardrobe, Alison," he remarked, "looked to me very much like a Dutch seaman's garb. The hotel clerk informed me that quite a large package was left at Reception for Mr. Weston. It could well have contained the suit the suspect wore for his interview with the manager."

Alison Aubrey laid down her fork momentarily beside her typically Swedish dish of spiced meat balls with red whortleberries.

"What you are suggesting, George, is that the suspect disguised himself as a sailor to effect his escape from Amsterdam, and that a change of clothes was waiting for him here in Stockholm, at Hotel Malmo?"

"If so, it raises some very interesting points," her colleague said. "Namely, that a third party probably booked the hotel room in advance, and quite possibly also made the appointment with Stig Lagerqvist."

"But why would the suspect risk leaving his original clothes at the hotel?" she asked, resuming her meal.

"He would hardly have taken them with him for a bank interview," George Mason said. "Besides, he had no further use for them. And remember, this guy is supremely confident. He will have no idea his movements are being shadowed."

"These meat balls are very tasty," Alison said, briefly changing the subject. "And I just love the berries."

"They serve them with most meat dishes," her colleague remarked. "In fact, berry-picking is one of the main industries here."

"I expect they grow wild, in the forests and on the mountain slopes."

"In the most inaccessible places, no doubt."

"Do we leave matters in the hands of the local police now?" the detective sergeant then asked.

George Mason nodded.

"We've achieved our main objective," he replied, "which was to establish a link between all three incidents. Chief Inspector Harrington will be expecting us to report back to him, so we must return to London tomorrow morning, much as I would have liked to see more of Stockholm. I like the way the ocean liners come right into the heart of the city."

His companion nodded agreement and scanned the dessert menu.

"Have we now established for certain the existence of a third party?" she eventually asked.

"The hidden hand?" he replied. "In the sense that someone may be planning the suspect's itinerary, booking hotel rooms and providing changes of clothing, yes. I should say it is quite possible that Milovan Piric is acting as someone's agent. A hired assassin, in fact."

"That third party presumably also being the source of the intriguing quotations?"

"Business is other people's money?" he remarked. "What do you make of that, Alison, as our resident riddle solver?"

The young officer returned an ironic smile, not quite sure how to take that remark.

"It could mean," she ventured, "that some people prefer to risk other people's money, rather than their own, for financial gain. Fund managers, for example."

George Mason glanced up from the remains of his grilled turbot, amazed at her perspicacity.

"Spot on, Sergeant!" he exclaimed. "I imagine it could mean exactly that."

"Or it could mean, on the other hand, that you have to make a sale, either of goods or services, relying on other people – the general public, no less - to come up with the money."

"Also quite plausible," her colleague conceded. "All commercial transactions boil down to money, in the end."

A ship's siren loudly pierced the air. Mason glanced through the restaurant window, to watch the approach of a large passenger vessel.

Alison was more interested in food.

"Think I'll try the cloudberry cheesecake," she said, quietly pleased that she had made a good impression.

"I'll settle for a liqueur coffee," Mason said. "When we're through here, we could take a stroll along the harbor and look at the boats. It'll be daylight for another hour yet. We might spot some British freighters."

"A great idea!" an enthusiastic Alison replied.

CHAPTER NINE

"What have you come up with so far, Inspector,"
Bill Harrington testily enquired at their brief
conference two days later, "after traveling half-way
across Europe at the taxpayer's expense?"

George Mason bridled inwardly at his superior's
typical sarcasm. He did not react, aware that the
department was operating under financial
constraints and that the Superintendent was
looking for economies.

"I'm reasonably convinced in my own mind that
these incidents are all related to the mortgage
industry," he said. "Possible suspects include the
ex-S.A.S. officer Paul Richardson, who had both
motive and opportunity, being in Amsterdam the
morning Willem de Vries was shot. Our other
possibility is Walter Cornelius, about whom we
know very little. He has so far proved impossible to
trace. The New Hampshire police are continuing
their enquiries."

"Purely circumstantial evidence, in other
words?"

"So far, yes," George Mason conceded.

"Anything else?"

"We now know for certain that the person who
fired the shots was Milovan Piric. He has left his

signature at each scene, in the form of a literary quotation."

"Is that a vindication of the modern education system, Inspector, that hit-men go around quoting Shakespeare?"

"Well," Mason laughingly replied, "if not the Bard of Avon, then certainly Somerset Maugham and Wallace Stevens, to name just two of the sources."

"And you are expecting me to swallow the notion that some ex-army type with a grudge against the banking industry has come up with this idea off his own bat?"

"That's one of the most intriguing aspects of the case," Mason said. "And we have as yet no convincing explanation for it. But we are fairly certain that Piric had a contact in Stockholm."

"Are you sure it wasn't his girlfriend?"

"Detective Sergeant Aubrey suggested that as one possible explanation of a torn note found in a discarded jacket in a hotel room booked under the name of Brad Weston."

"But you don't agree?"

"Both Kommissar Ahlgren and I thought it might have some connection with the attack on Stig Lagerqvist. The note seemed as if it could be directing Piric to The Old Post Office in Gamla Stan, the oldest part of Stockholm where Vardagsbank is also situated, possibly to pick up further instructions, poste restante."

"Pure supposition, Inspector," Harrington countered. "But it does raise the possibility that the Serb was acting on someone else's orders. That someone could be a more educated person who's playing games with the police, issuing these calling cards, as it were, as a kind of taunt."

"That possibility had not escaped me," George Mason said.

"So how do you see your next move?"

"There's a curious sort of pattern to these crimes, Chief Inspector," the other explained. "For a start, they have always occurred on a Friday morning, with a two-week interval between the first two incidents and a full month between the second and third."

"So you think you can predict when the next one will occur?"

"I can almost certainly predict the target."

Bill Harrington reached into the bottom drawer of his desk and drew out a bottle of Glenlivet. As his morning coffee had just arrived, he poured himself a tot to chase it with, without offering it.

"That's a big step forward, Inspector," he said, after a while, "if you're sure of your ground."

"The first three victims were all co-owners of Rollrock Ridge, the resort development in the White Mountains of New Hampshire. Urpo Koivonen, manager of Karelia Pankki in Helsinki, is the fourth registered owner. The four bankers – I learned this only yesterday from Donald Dinwiddie – are also registered at Companies House here in

London as the new owners of The Derwent Club in the Lake District."

"These bankers are being liquidated one by one?" the senior officer asked, in grave concern.

"Seems like some kind of vendetta," Mason said.

"Did the note you discovered contain a signature, by any chance?"

"In part only, since it was torn up. It was either Ja___ or Jo___. It does not seem to fit any of the names that have come up so far in this enquiry."

"Then you have your work cut out, Inspector. Now that you have come so far, I'll inform Superintendent Manwaring that I'm keeping you on the case for the time being. Now, if you'll excuse me, I have a deal of paperwork to attend to."

George Mason took the hint and returned to his own office with a sense of satisfaction that his efforts thus far were not unappreciated in the senior ranks. He would be very loath to quit the case, now that he had made some headway. Picking up the phone, he dialed International Directory Enquiries. Within minutes, he had the number of the Helsinki City Police. He quickly placed a call and asked to speak with Major Viljo Forsenius, who had assisted him some years back on an investigation into the disappearance of an English translator.

"Inspector Mason," came an upbeat voice over the line. "How are things with you, after all this time?"

"Can't complain," the detective replied, heartened to hear the familiar voice. "And with you?"

"Never better."

"And the family?"

"My wife Soili is keeping well and has returned to part-time teaching at Kotka Lyceum. Our son Pekka is in his final year at Helsinki University, reading biology. Time you paid us another visit, Inspector."

George Mason recalled with pleasure the invitation the Finnish officer had extended to him, during the course of his earlier investigation, to visit his home between Helsinki and Kotka for a sauna evening followed by dinner.

"That may very well be on the cards," he replied.

"Another missing Englishman, Inspector?"

"More likely, a case of murder."

"You can't be serious, Inspector."

"I'll give you the facts, Major, in so far as I know them and leave it to your judgment how to proceed."

"Fire away. I'm listening."

"There may well be, from what we have so far gleaned from an investigation currently in hand, an attempt on the life of the manager of Karelia Pankki, Urpo Koivonen."

"Urpo Koivonen?" Forsenius gasped, in evident surprise. "Why, I know him well. We belong to the same Rotary Chapter. Last March, he was runner-up in our annual ice-fishing tournament."

"Did you know that he had a major interest in an American resort development called Rollrock Ridge?"

"I think he has mentioned something along those lines, yes."

"Get this, Major. His three co-owners have all been shot. Only one of them is still alive, in a hospital in Amsterdam, and even he may not recover."

"There was a report the other day in our leading broadsheet, Helsingin Sanomat, concerning a shooting incident in Stockholm. The victim was indeed a bank manager, as I recall."

"It was the third in a series of similar attacks," the detective explained, "perpetrated by a fugitive called Milovan Piric. He may be heading your way."

"Do you have a full description?" the Major asked, with growing concern.

"Late forties, of medium height, with blond hair and a darker beard. In Stockholm he was reported to be wearing a light-blue business suit."

"How did he gain access to the bank?"

"Using a pseudonym, he had a prior appointment to discuss a mortgage loan. He was admitted to the manager's office by the receptionist, Liv Blofield, where he fired a single fatal shot. If you need fuller details on that incident, contact Kommissar Ahlgren of the Stockholm Police. He is actively seeking the suspect in Sweden where, of course, he may still be."

"I shall get in touch with the Kommissar right away, Inspector. But do you have a time-frame for Helsinki?"

"From what we have learned so far, from the pattern of previous incidents, you could probably expect a visit from Milovan Piric on the morning of Friday, May 26. Failing that, you should be on full alert the following Friday, June 2. You may well have received through Interpol a portrait of him in connection with a crime he committed in Hungary; but he has since altered his appearance. Ask your friend Koivonen to take particular note of any appointment booked on or around those dates by a man using a British or American surname."

"I'll do that, Inspector Mason," the Finn promised. "And thanks for the tip-off. I shall contact you immediately in the event of any developments. I shall also warn the manager and his staff to watch out for an individual fitting your description, and to be constantly on their guard."

"It may save his life," George Mason said, ringing off.

*

Milovan Piric prepared to leave Marienhamn on the morning of May 18, having spent the past week lying low in the seclusion of the Oland Islands, while taking advantage of local amenities. Not knowing what to expect on arrival, he was intrigued to discover a group of large, prosperous islands surrounded by hundreds of skerries, outcrops of rock in the Baltic too small to support habitation. Public transport was limited to a bus service linking the main settlements and there was a noticeable lack of motor cars, many islanders preferring to travel by bicycle now that the winter was behind them. At Hotel Cecilie, which offered comfortable if rustic accommodation and a first-rate sauna, he was able to rent a cycle for the week, as a way of keeping in shape and visiting some of the tourist sites. Shipping had long been the main industry, and he had cycled over to Berghamn on the west coast to view the clipper Pommern, which had seen service up to World War 2, carrying Australian wheat to Britain. He had been surprised, and a little put out, to learn from Jason's recent communication that his next assignment was scheduled for May 19, exactly one week after Stockholm; he would have preferred a longer stay in this low-key environment.

Having shaved off his beard, dyed his hair darker and donned the olive-green corduroy jacket left for him in a parcel at Reception, he packed his few belongings and went down to the dining-room for his standard breakfast of orange juice, rye porridge and locally-smoked herring. While awaiting service, he scanned the German-language newspaper that the hotel shipped from the mainland during the tourist season, since most foreign visitors sailed north across the Baltic from old Hansa ports like Bremen and Hamburg. Having noted that no progress was reported regarding the fatal shooting of a Swedish bank manager, he turned to the sports section to check how his favorite soccer team, Moscow Dynamos, were performing in the European Cup. Suppressing a sigh of disappointment at their defeat by Chelsea, the London borough where he had first met Jason, he took out the latter's letter and re-read it to make sure he had not missed something.

Everything seemed straightforward enough and he had no reason to doubt that, as on previous occasions, the assignment would go like clockwork. An appointment with the manager of Karelia Pankki, Urpo Koivonen, had already been set up for him in the name of a German couple called Gunther, in case the police should, by some improbable feat of detection, be on the look-out for a single male with an English surname, the ploy he had successfully used at Vardagsbank in Stockholm.

On arrival at the premises, situated on Mikonkatu, he was to explain to the receptionist that his wife, Frau Gunther, had an indisposition, but that she had insisted he proceed with the interview. The Serb refolded the letter and chuckled to himself. Jason considered all the angles and left nothing to chance. He tackled his hearty breakfast with a robust appetite from his recent outdoor activity, observing with interest the groups of early-season tourists at nearby tables, most of them dressed for sailing, hiking or cycling. Responding to their polite greetings, he was at the same time careful to avoid being drawn into extended conversation.

After his meal, he checked out of the hotel and made his way to the ferry terminal where an elegant blue-and-white vessel of the Silja Line was berthed. He noted its name, the Allotar, as he joined the stream of passengers mounting the gangway, securing a seat in the forward lounge, where coffee and light refreshments were being served. The vessel pulled promptly away from the quay at 10.15 a.m. By early afternoon, it was making its way through the vast archipelago Finns modestly refer to as 'the rock garden', bound for Turku, the former capital of Finland on the south-western tip of the country. Captivated by the sight of so many wooded islands, many with small summer cabins, Milovan Piric quit the lounge and strolled the decks, declining offers by a group of Americans to take part in a game of quoits. By late afternoon, the stark silhouette of Turku's medieval castle rose on the skyline; an hour later, the Allotar berthed in the compact harbor.

Transport to Helsinki was already waiting on the busy quay. Following a two-hour journey through rolling farmland, he arrived at his destination, conscious that this was to be his last assignment. A room had been booked for him at Hotel Kivi on Annankatu, a short street just across from the bus station. After checking in, he consulted the rough street-plan Jason had drawn for him and discovered that Karelia Pankki was around the corner from his hotel, on Mikonkatu. On his way out, he noted its precise location and turned his mind to food, not having eaten much since breakfast. It was early evening by now and the restaurants he passed seemed fully occupied. Turning into a narrow alley off Station Square, he at length found an establishment that perfectly suited his need for anonymity. On entering, he joined a small queue leading to an electronic menu board with a button against each item. The food service was completely screened from the dining area. Patrons pressed their chosen button and pushed a tray along the counter to a serving hatch, which opened and then promptly shut as each meal emerged.

When his turn came, Milovan Piric had no idea how to read the Finnish menu. What an impossible language it was! Unlike any European tongue that he knew. He took pot luck, pressed the button beside one of the pricier items and moved his tray towards the hatch. Service was quick. Within minutes, he was seated in a quiet corner of the restaurant addressing a reindeer steak, with baked potato and mixed salad. Not a single member of the restaurant staff appeared for the duration of the meal. This aspect greatly appealed to him, as did the reserve of his fellow-diners arriving from offices and shops in the city center. The local patrons did not even converse among themselves, being content to read books or newspapers as they ate. He had read somewhere that the Finns were a taciturn folk.

On finishing his food, he took advantage of the fine evening to stroll down to South Harbor to watch the freighters prepare for overnight departure, winding his way back to the city center by way of the tree-fringed Brunnspark. Over a nightcap in the hotel bar, he mentally reviewed procedures for the following day. The bank would open at 8.30 a.m., his appointment being scheduled shortly after that, in the name of Herr and Frau Gunther. What a nice surprise was in store for Urpo Koivonen, he mused. Of more concern to him at this precise moment, however, was his escape route after the event. Jason had advised him that main transit venues like Seutola Airport, the railway station and the main ports were to be avoided. He was to take a taxi from Station Square as far as Tampere, an industrial town in central Finland, and entrain there to Finland's northern frontier.

Once there, he could cross into Sweden without border controls and take the train from Boden to Trondheim on the Norwegian coast, on switching to a cross-country train at Sundsvall. From Trondheim, he would soon reach Oslo, where he would be home and dry. From there, air services and shipping lines could take him anywhere in the world he chose to go. With his last installment of the fee, which Jason had left for him at Hotel Kivi, he was now 100,000 euros to the good, enough to buy a medium-sized farm. He retired early, in a contented frame of mind.

*

Urpo Koivonen rose early on the morning of May 19, showered, dressed for business and went into breakfast in the kitchen of his spacious flat in Tapiola, an island suburb in the Gulf of Finland. His wife Paivi, a willowy blonde several years his junior, had already prepared his customary simple meal consisting of juice, muesli with yoghurt and fresh fruit, and coffee. It being Friday, his thoughts centered more on weekend leisure activities than on the daily grind of the banking world.

"Do we have anything planned for tomorrow?" he asked his wife, who did not join him at table, but busied herself watering house plants on the sills and the open balcony.

"The Lehtinens have invited us aboard their yacht for lunch and an afternoon's sailing," she replied, in a tone of voice that conveyed keen anticipation. "And your son Kimo will be home from college on Sunday, for the start of his spring break."

"Do they spend any time at all on course work these days?" Urpo rhetorically enquired. "The fees they charge are certainly steep enough."

"It was just the same in your day," Paivi tartly replied, "but you have conveniently forgotten. Kimo works very hard at his studies and is sure to earn himself a good degree."

"He will need one, in the current employment climate."

With that, the bank manager fell to consuming his light meal, after which he took up Helsingin Sanomat to scan the headlines. One particular news item immediately drew his attention.

"Did you read, Paivi," he asked, "that the Swedish Police now have a suspect in the Stig Lagerqvist case?"

"Haven't had time to look at the newspaper yet," she said, momentarily returning to the kitchen. "How is Stig's wife taking it?"

"Very hard, I believe," her husband replied. "But I haven't had chance to speak with Birgit personally."

"Poor thing. How dreadful for her. I must try to get over to see her when Kimo is back at college."

"That's probably a good idea," he said. "Birgit would greatly appreciate it. It appears from this article that the suspect, as yet unnamed, is thought to have a military background and to be armed and dangerous. Present whereabouts unknown."

Urpo Koivonen had not mentioned to his wife that he had received a phone call from Major Viljo Forsenius, a fellow-member of the Rotary Club, for fear of causing her alarm. Forsenius had started to explain to him that, according to a Scotland Yard detective who had been following the case, the attack on Lagerqvist was the third in a series of crimes against the co-owners of Rollrock Ridge. That was not news to him, since Alderney

Mortgages had already apprised him of the death of Conrad Fields and the serious condition of Willem de Vries, events which had not been reported in the Finnish press, and which he had therefore been able to conceal from Paivi. The Major had indicated that plainclothes officers would be stationed at Karelia Pankki during the week commencing May 22, in such a way as to appear like regular customers. The critical date was thought to be Friday, May 26, but the police were leaving nothing to chance, and the manager was to take particular note in the meantime of appointments booked by a single male using an English or American surname.

Koivonen had considered that a bit odd. Appointments were usually made well in advance. A review of his diary for the last week of May, which he had made before leaving the bank yesterday, did not reveal any single names at all. All prospective mortgage clients were married couples, none of them with Anglo-Saxon names. He had taken the precaution, after Paivi had gone to bed last night, of retrieving his old army pistol from the garage, cleaning it and placing it loaded in his briefcase. He would keep it by him in his desk drawer, police presence or no police presence, from now on, until there was news of the gunman's arrest. Bidding his wife good-bye, he descended to the basement garage and eased himself into his year-old Nexus for the half-hour commute by the shore of the Gulf of Finland. As he drove, the fate of his associate in Rollrock Ridge was uppermost in his mind. The Lagerqvists had been long-term friends, whom they occasionally visited for yachting trips among the skerries off Sweden's east coast. They returned the compliment by inviting the Swedish couple to the summer cabin they owned by Lake Saimaa, for swimming, rod fishing and sauna evenings.

The deaths of Conrad Fields and Stig Lagerqvist had serious business as well as personal implications, he reflected, as he slowed down on joining heavier traffic through the suburb of Kulosaari. The ownership of the White Mountains resort had been set up under a legal device known as Concurrent Estate. It meant that, on the death of any given co-owner, his share of the property passed automatically to the surviving owners, rather than to the deceased's heirs. Were Willem de Vries also to die, he, Urpo Koivonen, would become sole proprietor of a resort property worth close to three million dollars, the bulk of which was in hock to the mortgage company. There was no way a single owner like himself could repay such a loan. His best hope now was for de Vries to make a full recovery, so that they could work out the financial angles between them. A joint ownership, with the resources of their two banks behind them, might just be feasible, if they could persuade their respective boards of directors to back the scheme.

He was in a fairly upbeat frame of mind when he entered Karelia Pankki, greeting the receptionist,

Riitta Puntilla, in his customary cheery manner and looking forward to getting through the day quickly, with the prospect of a day's sailing with the Lehtinens on the morrow. Pentti Lehtinen was an old friend from his army days; his much younger wife, Orvokki, whom Pentti had married two years after a protracted divorce, was a tiresome social climber whom his friend had met on a four-day Baltic cruise to Tallinn and Riga. Paivi seemed to get along with her well enough, which was all that really mattered. She made allowances for Orvokki's occasional gaucheries and eased her entry into a middle-class Tapiola social club centered on bridge, keep-fit sessions at the new swimming pool, skiing over the frozen sea in winter, and classes in French cuisine. Entering his ground-floor office, he sat down and consulted his diary, after placing his pistol in the bottom drawer of his desk.

Riitta Puntilla soon afterwards brought him his morning coffee, to refresh him after his commute. Half an hour later, she rang through from Reception to inform him that the first of his mortgage clients had arrived. The bank manager consulted his diary.

"Herr und Frau Gunther?" he casually enquired.

"Only Herr Gunther has arrived," she replied. "He explained that his wife was indisposed – some minor ailment, apparently – but that she did not wish her husband to forego the appointment."

"Describe this Herr Gunther to me."

"Medium height, clean-shaven, with dark-brown hair. Fortyish, I should say."

Milovan Piric, clad in the olive sports jacket Jason had left for him at Hotel Kivi, stood there totally bemused by the sound of the fluent Finnish spoken by the receptionist, of which he understood not one word. Although Finnish was related to Hungarian, of which he had a smattering from occasional visits to Budapest, he detected no obvious similarities.

Urpo Koivonen pondered the situation for a few moments. Hadn't Major Forsenius warned specifically against visits by single males? Determined to take no chances, he withdrew his army pistol from the drawer and held it across his lap below the level of the desk-top, so that a visitor would be unaware of it. He then instructed Riitta Puntilla to show the man through.

The Serb strode purposefully towards the manager's office, knocked and entered.

"Herr Gunther?" Koivonen genially enquired, without rising. "I was expecting to meet also with your wife. You are both interested in mortgage finance?"

"My wife is indisposed," Piric replied, wondering why the manager remained seated, instead of rising to greet him, thus making a better target.

"Please take a seat," the Finn then said.

The visitor sat down facing the manager across the desk.

"I have a letter of introduction," he began, looking the manager straight in the eye while reaching under his jacket.

Koivonen's alert gaze followed the movement and he soon caught a glint of metal. Instantly raising his right arm, he aimed his pistol squarely at the intruder's upper torso and fired a single shot, as the Serb's weapon was barely clear of its holster. Piric, with a look of agonized disbelief, clutched his chest and fell forward across the polished desk. Riitta Puntilla heard the shot and came running in, screaming when she saw the half-recumbent body.

"Pull yourself together, woman," he said, controlledly. "Call Major Forsenius at once. Then ring for an ambulance."

The receptionist rushed back to her post and telephoned Police Headquarters. Within fifteen minutes Major Viljo Forsenius, accompanied by two junior officers, had covered the short drive from South Harbor to Mikonkatu. A more composed Riitta Puntilla led them to the manager's office.

"You all right, Urpo?" the Major enquired, with a concerned glance at his Rotary associate, who had placed his gun in plain view on the blood-stained desk, while his receptionist hovered nervously by the door.

"A bit shaken, to tell the truth," Koivonen replied, "but nothing worse than that."

"Tell me exactly what happened."

"I was expecting to interview a German couple by the name of Gunther, regarding a residential mortgage. At the appointed time, a single male introducing himself as Herr Gunther arrived at Reception.   He explained that his wife was indisposed, but that he still wished to keep the appointment."

"Mrs. Puntilla sent him through?"

"After advising me of the circumstances, yes. From what you told me the other day, I was immediately on my guard. The intruder reached for his weapon within moments of entering, but I had taken the precaution of arriving prepared. That is my old service pistol you see there on the desk."

The Major glanced from the weapon to its owner, with an appreciative nod.

"But the attack was not expected to take place until next week," he remarked. "Inspector Mason, of Scotland Yard Special Branch, seemed fairly confident of that. He was fitting it into some sort of pattern he had discerned on the basis of similar attacks in the recent past."

"He was certainly right about the day, it being a Friday," Urpo Koivonen acknowledged. "But the exact date may have been more difficult to predict. Realizing that, I took the precaution after your warning of coming to work armed, on the off-chance that something like this might occur."

"Good thinking, Urpo," Forsenius appreciatively remarked. "And a plus for your military training."

"Paivi will be intensely relieved."

"Shall I ring her for you, Sir?" Mrs. Puntilla asked. "Let her know you're all right?"

"I don't think so," came the terse reply. "It'll only alarm her. I'll call her myself later on, or perhaps I'll wait till I get home. It will dominate all the media this evening."

"Now what do we have here?" Forsenius said, turning to the corpse. "This individual should, according to Inspector George Mason, be a certain Milovan Piric. But we need positive identification. If you two officers will turn him over for me, let's see if he's carrying ID."

The sergeant and the corporal stepped forward and eased the still-warm corpse onto its back. The Major then reached into the inside jacket pocket and drew out a leather wallet. In it, he found a passport and a bank debit card.

"It's Milovan Piric all right," he announced. "He was obviously sure enough of himself not to disguise his identity."

"Now that they have abolished border controls within the European Union, wouldn't he have been able to go from one country to another without producing his passport?" the bank manager asked.

"That's an advantage the criminal has these days," the Major agreed. "With passport checks, he might have been apprehended much earlier."

The sound of an ambulance siren was heard in the street outside. Before the crew entered to transfer the body to the morgue, Viljo Forsenius quickly reached into the jacket side-pockets, withdrawing some loose change and a slip of paper.

"Seems to be a quotation of some kind," he remarked, on quickly scanning it. "Means nothing to me, but it may mean something to George Mason. I'll ring him soon as I get back to HQ. After the body is removed, Urpo, you can get this place cleaned up without delay. No need for forensics. In my report, I'll state that it was a clear case of self-defense. You behaved with admirable coolness in the circumstances."

With that, he took possession of the intruder's Ruger, placed it in a polythene bag and left the building followed by one of his colleagues. The other, more senior officer, he left in place to supervise removal of the body.

CHAPTER TEN

Later that day, on receiving a telephone call from Finland, George Mason went immediately to Chief Inspector Harrington to tell him the news.

"So the perpetrator of all these incidents has finally met his nemesis?" Harrington asked, with evident satisfaction.

"He was shot dead by the manager of Karelia Pankki earlier today."

"And you, of course, predicted the attempt?"

George Mason was dismissive.

"I accurately predicted that an attempt would be made on the life of Urpo Koivonen, and that it would take place on a Friday," he explained. "But I was a week out in my timing. I had anticipated May 26."

"But you did enough to forewarn the Finns, and to be forewarned is to be forearmed," the other said, in complimentary vein. "If it hadn't been for you, Inspector, Koivonen would now be a dead duck."

"Lucky for him he had the foresight to pack his army pistol. Knew how to use it, too, by all accounts."

"And you say the gunman has been positively identified?"

"Milovan Piric, as we have thought for some time now. Major Forsenius retrieved his passport from his jacket."

"Quite amazing that he was carrying valid ID around with him," Harrington considered. "Over-confident, no doubt."

"He was constantly on the move," his colleague said, "no doubt thinking he would always be one step ahead of the police, and that we would never connect incidents separated by both space and time."

"So we can take it that the case is now solved, can we, Inspector?" Harrington asked. "And that we can leave it to the Swedish and the Finnish police to do the mopping up?"

"I hardly think so, Chief Inspector," Mason countered. "And for this reason: I don't think Piric was acting alone. I have grown increasingly convinced in the course of this inquiry that he was a hired assassin. This case is by no means over."

Bill Harrington said nothing for a few moments. He looked searchingly at his colleague, while his right hand hovered in the vicinity of the desk drawer which housed his Glenlivet. Resisting the urge, he eventually said:

"It's not going to be easy to square this with the Superintendent, but I'll try my best. I'll go and see him straight away, before he leaves for a Whitehall conference. Call me back in about an hour."

"Have you heard any news regarding the Dutchman, Willem de Vries?"

"He's out of danger, so I understand," Harrington said. "Due to leave hospital within days and continue his convalescence at home."

"Thank goodness for that," Mason said. "That limits the damage to two killings. Tragic enough for those involved, certainly, but it could have been much worse."

"Thanks to you, Inspector," the Chief Inspector generously allowed. "And to your ability to find a common thread running through these incidents. I'll see that both the Commissioner and the Superintendent are made fully aware of the facts."

"I'd much appreciate that, Chief Inspector."

On regaining his own office, an upbeat George Mason placed a call to National Indemnity, asking to speak with the Assistant Manager.

"Jeffries," came a formal voice over the line.

"George Mason, of Scotland Yard," the detective said. "How are things with you?"

"Slowly getting back to normal," Jeffries explained. "We're interviewing next week for a replacement for Conrad Fields. Several well-qualified candidates have applied for the job."

"I have some news for you, Mr. Jeffries. The culprit in the incident which took place at your premises in March has been identified as Milovan Piric, a former non-commissioned officer in the Serbian Army."

"You have been able to arrest him?" the Assistant Manager optimistically enquired.

"He was shot dead earlier today," the detective said, "while attempting a similar attack on the manager of Karelia Pankki in Helsinki."

"You don't say so, Inspector!" the other exclaimed. "That's a remarkable turn-up for the book. But I understand that Stig Lagerqvist was not so fortunate."

"Did you know Mr. Lagerqvist personally?" Mason asked.

"He visited London once or twice late last year. I think he had some private business with Mr. Fields. I did have the opportunity to meet him very briefly, but other than that I had no dealings with him. I am not much involved in the banking side of the business, just the insurance, as I explained earlier."

"Just thought I'd keep you up-to-date," the detective then said. "If there are further developments, which there may well be, I shall let you know."

"That sounds quite promising, Inspector. More strength to your arm."

"And, by the way, it was the manager of Karelia Pankki, Urpo Koivonen, who shot dead the intruder. I don't suppose you knew him, too?"

"Afraid not," Jeffries replied. "But I should certainly like to."

*

The Finnair jet carrying George Mason and Alison Aubrey touched down at Seutola Airport just after six o'clock the following day. Alison Aubrey had been given very short notice the previous afternoon, following Harrington's meeting with Superintendent Mulholland. The senior officer had demurred about the expense, but felt in the end that it would be useful experience for the younger officer to follow the case to its conclusion. Mulholland was an advocate of equal opportunity, keen to see more females rise up through the ranks. His wife Glynis, a former lecturer in criminology, now held a senior post in the Essex Constabulary.

Major Viljo Forsenius was at the airport in person, greeting them cordially before ushering them into the rear seat of his car for the drive to Hotel Kivi. Once there, he allowed them time to check in and freshen up, before joining them for dinner in the hotel restaurant, tastefully decorated with Lapp motifs such as reindeer antlers, stuffed lynx and wolverine. In one corner stood a pair of antique wooden skis originally used on the Lapland fells.

"Like old times, Inspector," the Finn remarked, as they sat down to read the menu. He was referring to their collaboration in the case of John Ormond, the English translator who some years back had gone missing from Helsinki. "Except that on that occasion you were here in the depths of winter."

"Don't I know it, Major!" Mason vehemently replied. "Trudging through snowbound city streets, skiing over frozen bays. It beats me how you manage to maintain normal life in such extreme conditions. In England, just a few inches of snow are guaranteed to cause maximum chaos and disruption."

"Habituation," the Major drily commented, "combined with our native capacity for endurance, which we fondly refer to as sisu."

"Might sauna-bathing have something to do with that?" Alison Aubrey artfully suggested, as they placed orders for roast elk.

Forsenius returned an odd look, unsure if she wasn't ribbing him.

"You should try the Finnish bath for yourself, Alison, while we're here," George Mason diplomatically intervened. "They're sure to have one here in the hotel."

"But you wouldn't be getting the full treatment," the Finn interjected. "It's the roll in the snow afterwards that's the real toughener."

"I'll take your word for it, Major," Alison said. "But I think I'd settle for a warm shower instead. That is, if I can pluck up courage to try the real thing. I imagine the Finnish sauna is far hotter than the one we have at our keep-fit club."

The small talk continued during the course of the meal, Alison asking all manner of questions about Finnish life, the status of women and contemporary fashions. Viljo Forsenius was obviously gratified at her keen interest in a country that he realized was little-known beyond its own borders.

"You should speak to my wife, Soili, about feminine issues," he said. "I was hoping she would join us for dinner, but she couldn't face the long drive from Kotka after her day's work. This evening, I shall stay over at my son's place in Kulosaari. Tomorrow being Sunday, I shall pick you up here at your hotel after breakfast and show you some of the sights. We can't make a useful start on your case until Monday, in any event."

The Scotland Yard pair exchanged compliant glances: a more relaxed day, in the hectic context of recent events, was welcome.

"Bill Harrington certainly won't be any the wiser," George Mason wryly observed, mainly for his young colleague's benefit.

"The assailant, in any case, is lying dead in the city morgue," Forsenius said. "It only remains for you to tie up the loose ends."

George Mason wondered if that was going to be as straightforward as the Finn suggested, but he reserved comment.

With that, they rounded off the meal with dessert and coffee. Left to themselves after the Finnish officer had departed for the outer suburbs, they explored the immediate environs of the hotel for a while, to stretch their legs, before repairing to the hotel bar as it grew dark, for a nightcap and an hour or so of Finnish television. The movie channel was showing a dubbed version of The Bourne Supremacy, one of Mason's favorite films, which they picked up half-way through.

Major Forsenius returned just after ten o'clock the following morning, after the Scotland Yard pair had tackled a breakfast of rye porridge and cold cuts, without much noticing a man vaguely resembling the actor George Peppard hurriedly finishing his meal on the far side of the restaurant. The Major, being very proud of his city, suggested a brief tour to take in the Parliament Building, the University, the National Theater and the Railway Station, famously designed by Eliel Saarinen. An hour later, the trio were standing on Observatory Hill, a vantage point giving panoramic views of the Finnish capital, with South Harbor in the foreground.

"That's the Lutheran Cathedral," Forsenius said, indicating the large white edifice dominating the scene.

"And what is the large red-brick church with the onion domes, over there on the right?" an inquisitive Alison Aubrey asked.

"That's the Ouspensky Cathedral."

"Russian Orthodox," George Mason put in.

"After Lutheranism," the Finn explained, "it is the next major denomination, stemming from the days when Finland was a Russian grand duchy."

"A status which ended in 1917?" Mason asked.

"You know your Finnish history, Inspector," Forsenius complimented him. "During the Bolshevik Revolution, Finland declared her independence from Russia and maintained it, with some precarious moments, throughout World War 2 and the Cold War period."

"Which thankfully has now ended," Alison remarked.

"We are now fully-fledged members of the European Union, with a prosperous economy and a common currency."

"What is the building on that island in the middle of the bay?" asked Alison, who was keen to take in everything.

"That's the headquarters of the Yacht Club," the major informed her. "And beyond that, guarding the entrance to the harbor, is the island fortress of Suomenlinna. It was constructed of granite blocks over two hundred years ago and has heavy cannon facing out to sea."

"An impressive defensive structure," George Mason opined.

"I hate to say this," the Finn then said, with mock apology, "but those same guns were trained on British ships during the Crimean War."

"While Finland was under Russian rule?" the bemused Englishman asked. "We shall have to overlook that aberration."

The remark produced general mirth, and on that note of good humor they returned to the car and were soon heading out into the hinterland, through rolling farmland, placid lakes and dense forest. After a drive of about twenty-five miles, their guide turned into a country lane and pulled up outside a large lakeside dwelling.

"This is Lake Tuusula," Forsenius explained. "And the house is Ainola, the former home of Jean

Sibelius, our most celebrated composer, whose music is particularly associated with Finnish independence."

"Finlandia?" Mason queried.

"And much more besides. Sibelius based a lot of his music on the Finnish national epic, Kalevala, and on Finnish history and mythology."

"You can almost sense the presence of the wood-sprites here," Alison remarked. "It's so remote from city life."

"When he first moved here with his wife Aino," the Finn explained, "it was virtually undisturbed, pristine countryside. The perfect milieu, in fact, for his unique style and temperament."

"May we go inside?" Alison then asked.

"By all means," their guide replied. "Ainola was given to the nation in 1974 by Sibelius's daughters, to provide a permanent memorial to their father."

Leaving the car, they walked along the garden path and stopped part-way before a marble slab in the center of the lawn. It bore the name of the composer, who died in 1957, and that of his wife, indicating that she had survived him by several years.

"They wished to be buried on their own property," Forsenius explained, "since it was here that Sibelius composed most of his music, after a riotous youth in Helsinki. His first ambition was to be a concert violinist, but at some point he changed course. A serious illness had something to do with it, if I remember correctly."

"Lucky for music lovers that he did," George Mason observed. "His works are very popular in England and America; but not so much in France and Italy, I believe."

"Perhaps a bit too somber for the Latin temperament," the Finn drily observed.

On entering, they visited the study housing the composer's library, manuscripts and grand piano, which was said to have been gifted to him on his fiftieth birthday, implying that he could never afford to buy one as he struggled to raise a large family and gain recognition. The remaining rooms were closed off, being readied for the official re-opening after the long winter, so the police trio explored the rambling grounds, complete with sauna hut and workshop. After a pleasant hour or so in the shadow of great music, they drove on to the nearby town of Jarvenpaa, to view buildings designed by the famous architect, Alvar Aalto. They then took light refreshment at a roadside inn, before returning to the capital. Viljo Forsenius dropped them at Hotel Kivi and left to rejoin his wife at Kotka, a busy timber port some miles east of Helsinki. The Scotland Yard pair were to meet him again first thing Monday morning at Police HQ facing South Harbor, a fifteen-minute walk from their hotel.

*

That evening, Jason was reading Helsingin Sanomat, the city's main broadsheet, in the bar of Hotel Kivi, an establishment popular with foreign visitors, where he had been staying for the last few days. His attention suddenly focused on a couple who had just entered. He heard them ordering drinks in English before crossing to a table in a corner of the room, recalling that they had been here the previous evening to watch television, and that they had also appeared in the restaurant this morning, just as he was finishing breakfast. Their presence intrigued him, since he had met no English speakers during his short stay in the Finnish capital. It briefly occurred to him to introduce himself, but something about the man's aspect dissuaded him. To Jason, he had the gravitas one associates more readily with public officials. He also seemed quite a bit older than his attractive young companion with the gamine hairstyle, who had ordered a spritzer to the other's whiskey-and-soda.

Lowering his newspaper, he watched them unobserved for a while, before concluding from their general demeanor that they were probably not man and wife. It was a bit early in the season for tourists, he considered, finally deciding that they were most likely a business couple, a company executive of some sort with his secretary. He was aware that Finland did a lot of foreign trade with her new European partners, not just in timber, cellulose and paper products, but also in modern technologies, particularly cell-phones.

Returning to his newspaper, he became absorbed in the account of the attack on the manager of Karelia Pankki. The police had done remarkably well, he reluctantly allowed, to identify Milovan Piric so quickly. Piric had evidently not covered his tracks carefully enough, and he already had, on his own admission, something of a police record. Reflecting on the matter, he felt little sympathy for his dead hit-man. In some ways, Piric's demise was a good thing. The authorities would now consider that they had solved their case and that should be the end of the matter. He felt supremely confident that he could not in any way be linked to the attacks: there was simply no trail. The Serb had clearly been clean out of luck to confront a target who was also armed, apparently an ex-serviceman like himself.

But wasn't that, after all, an occupational hazard? Urpo Koivonen had probably read of the murder of Stig Lagerqvist and decided to take precautions, correctly figuring that attacks on three bank managers were not random events, but had a common thread, and that he could be next in line. Lucky for Koivonen, whose reprieve Jason considered temporary. It would be a simple enough matter to hire another agent on the Internet, who could also take care of unfinished business in Amsterdam. The police would sooner or later inform Willem de Vries of Piric's death, and all concerned would relax their guard.

Folding his newspaper, he returned to the bar to order a prawn-and-lettuce open sandwich. He hovered close enough to the English couple to catch snatches of their conversation. The man, in so far as he could tell, was expounding to his young companion on that curious English pursuit called cricket. Something about a test match against Australia. Putting them out of his mind, he collected his snack and returned to his table, musing as he ate about his wife, Arlene. She had walked out on him three months ago and was filing for a divorce he did not intend to contest. Arlene was the sort of woman who was perfectly happy when things were going well and she could buy expensive clothes, perfumes and jewelry. She was not a person who could make adjustments to her standard of living during a downturn and would probably end up re-marrying such as a stockbroker or an attorney.

She was still young and attractive enough to do so, and had a string of admirers in their social circle. She had married him at the peak of his career, probably as a good meal ticket, having survived a broken home and a single-parent upbringing on the wrong side of town. Before retiring for the night, he would give her a call and update himself on the latest legal developments. He would also pack his valise for his morning voyage by Silja Line across the Gulf of Finland, the eastern arm of the Baltic Sea, to Tallinn. Rising at length from his chair, he cast a final glance at the English couple. They were about to begin dinner.

CHAPTER ELEVEN

George Mason and Alison Aubrey left their hotel shortly after breakfast on Monday morning and headed up Mannerheim, the city's main street, dodging the trams as they crossed over and took a left turn by the Swedish Theater. It was a short walk from there, along tree-lined Esplanade, to the South Harbor, where the morning market was getting under way. Vendors from along the coast moored their small craft to the quay and began unloading their produce onto wooden stalls, where customers were starting to gather. As they were a few minutes ahead of their appointment with Major Forsenius, the two detectives allowed themselves a brief inspection, Alison being particularly intrigued at varieties of fish on offer. A steam engine pulling a large crane behind it suddenly came trundling along the rails to help unload a merchant vessel berthed in the deeper water. George Mason noted its name, Seagull, out of Liverpool. Helsinki, he decided, was much like Stockholm, in that ocean-going ships came into the heart of the city.

Viljo Forsenius greeted them cordially as they entered his Headquarter's office on the far side of the harbor.

"You were suggesting earlier, Inspector," he began, "that Milovan Piric had some sort of accomplice?"

"I'm going off cryptic notes left at the scene of each crime," Mason said.

"Then this should be of some interest to you," the Finn said, with an artful smile, as he fished from his pocket a crumpled slip of paper. "It was discovered when they went through Piric's clothing at the morgue."

Mason accepted it with an ironic look and read aloud: "They took some honey and plenty of money, wrapped up in a five-pound note."

"Edward Lear," Alison Aubrey said, at once.

"From The Owl and the Pussy-cat," her colleague agreed.

Major Forsenius looked on, bemused.

"Is there some significance to this jingle?" he asked.

"Edward Lear was a composer of nonsense verse," Mason explained. "He has always been very popular in England."

"A country not lacking in eccentrics," the Finn drily observed.

"This series of notes," Alison said, "seems to point to a person of some literary flair. We've already had Somerset Maugham, Wallace Stevens and another as yet unidentified quote."

"Maugham I am familiar with," the Major then said. "They made some good movies from his novels. The Razor's Edge, for example. It was shown on television, with Finnish sub-titles."

"We think this individual, whoever he is, moves around quite a lot," Mason added. "All we have to go off, however, is the letters Jo___, or possibly Ja___, written on a torn note left in the Stockholm hotel where Piric was staying under an assumed name the night before his attack on Lagerqvist."

"Then we have our work cut out, Inspector," Forsenius remarked. "Those letters could stand for any of a dozen names."

"I have been giving this matter some considerable thought," George Mason then said, "during the short time we have been in Finland. And it occurred to me that a fruitful field of enquiry might be the cultural scene. A music ensemble, for example, or a dance troupe. Something of that order. Perhaps even a circus, as an outside possibility."

The Finn slowly nodded in agreement.

"What you could be looking for, in fact, is some sort of touring group, or individual, whose presence in these northern cities coincides with the dates of the attacks."

"That's approximately what I was thinking," Mason replied.

"I'll check with Helsinki Arts. They should have up-to-date information, for advance publicity purposes."

He picked up the desk phone and dialed. There ensued an exchange in fluent Finnish, completely beyond the English pair. The Major made brief notes.

"There are several possibilities," he eventually announced. "First, there is a Czech modern jazz trio on tour here, hosted by Hotel Metropoli."

"The Czech Republic?" Alison mused aloud. "That's at least the correct general area."

"What Americans call the right ballpark?" Forsenius asked, keen to air his knowledge of idioms.

George Mason returned an indulgent smile.

"They're on the last leg of a Scandinavian tour," the Finn explained, "before returning to Prague via Berlin."

"That would exclude London and Amsterdam," Mason said, carefully checking the relevant dates, "where the first two attacks occurred."

"Afraid so."

"What else have you got?"

"There's a British string quartet also on tour. They're giving a matinee performance at the university this very afternoon. Their program includes readings from English poets."

"That looks a bit more promising than a Czech jazz trio," Mason said. "What time does it begin?"

"One o'clock," the Major informed him. "Tickets will be available at the door."

"How do we locate it?" Alison asked.

"Just walk along Alexander Street, until you pass the cathedral. You'll soon spot a large stone building on the right, with the words Helsingin

Yliopisto over the portico. I'd come with you, but I have to drive up to Lahti just now to investigate a domestic incident involving firearms. I won't be back in time. And, by the way, when you're through at the university, you could drop by the Swedish Theater and pick up a program for Arthur Miller's A View from the Bridge. It's being presented by Pro Thespis, a drama company also currently on a European tour."

"Do we call back here later?" Mason wanted to know.

"By all means," the Finn replied. "I shall be back here by four o'clock at the latest and shall be very interested in anything you have to report. Urpo Koivonen is a personal friend of mine. The last thing I want to risk is a second attempt on his life if, as you surmise, Milovan Piric was not the prime mover in this series of incidents."

The two detectives took leave of him and re-emerged into the strong spring sunlight with an hour or so to kill. The outdoor market was now in full swing, so they took the opposite direction to avoid the melee. Since his young colleague was interested in seeing examples of Finnish design, George Mason introduced her to Stockmann's, a department store that carried a broad range of ceramics, glassware and metalwork. While Alison was taking her time admiring the bold designs and striking colors, his eye was taken by carved wooden pictures depicting forest scenes, lakeside saunas and rural hearths. He could well imagine one on his living-room wall at home, but would Adele be as keen, he wondered? She had very different tastes in décor.

"I couldn't possibly leave Finland without an example of this beautiful glassware," Alison said, on re-joining him. "But they're quite pricey."

"Finnish design is world-famous," Mason said. "Textiles, ceramics, cutlery. You name it. They're in the top league, so you're paying for quality."

"I'll think about it," she pensively replied. "No need to decide right now."

"I say we go to The Three Counts restaurant on Mannerheim and grab a bite to eat before heading along Alexander Street. We can pick up a current program at the Swedish Theater on the way. It's directly opposite. "

Leaving Stockmann's empty-handed, they soon reached the low, circular building at the mouth of Esplanade. On entering the foyer, George Mason immediately noticed that the play bill had changed. A View from the Bridge was the previous week's production; the current one being Miss Julie by the Swedish dramatist, August Strindberg. Fortunately, the booking clerk still had Miller programs left over and willingly gave them one. Their brief errand completed, they crossed back over Mannerheim and entered the restaurant on the mezzanine floor of a multi-storey office block, joining the short queue at the self-service counter. They bought open sandwiches with coffee, finding a table by the window overlooking the late-morning scene with a point-duty policeman controlling the busy intersection.

"I came here quite often, while working on the John Ormond case," George Mason informed his companion as they took their seats, "because you can point to whatever you want to eat."

"To avoid having to decipher Finnish menus?" Alison asked.

"Precisely. It avoids making ghastly mistakes like raw, salted herring and curdled milk," he said, grimacing at the recollection. "Quite amazing what some people find edible."

"You're quite the seasoned traveler, aren't you, George?" Alison said, approvingly.

"It's just that I've learned from previous mistakes," came the wry reply.

While eating, they turned their attention to the theater program.

"This Pro Thespis group hails from America," Mason remarked. "They're apparently nearing the end of a major European tour, presenting a series of plays by Arthur Miller and Edward Albee. They have already played in several major cities."

"Does it give dates?" Alison asked.

"No, but the coincidence in venues seems interesting. I in fact went to watch a Miller play when I was in Amsterdam last month. Must have been this very same company, but its name had slipped my mind."

"That's quite a coincidence, George. Which play did you see?"

"All My Sons."

"I have only ever seen Focus, said to be his most controversial play, at London's South Bank Theater. Does the program list the cast?"

Mason shook his head.

"Unfortunately not," he replied. "But what strikes me, if this list of cities is the actual order of itinerary, is the longish gap between Amsterdam and Stockholm. That could be explained by performances in other places, such as Berlin, Copenhagen and Oslo."

"What exactly are you driving at, George?" Alison asked.

"The attacks on Willem de Vries and Stig Lagerqvist were exactly six weeks apart. Both of them took place on a Friday morning, which may just possibly coincide with the end of the play run in each of those cities."

"You are suggesting that a member of Pro Thespis may be behind these incidents?"

"I am merely pointing to a coincidence," Mason said. "We can't do anything without names, which is something we don't have. Nor do we have accurate dates, as of yet. I should like to know if Pro Thespis were in London in mid-March."

"You could easily find that out. Ring Bill Harrington."

"Later," he replied. "We should really be making our way to the university."

The young detective sergeant quickly finished her snack, nipped briefly into the restroom and rejoined her colleague, who was already in the street outside. They re-crossed Mannerheim, dodging the speeding trams, which had precedence over motor vehicles and pedestrians, and made their way down Alexander Street, named after a former Russian tsar. Entering the building, they bought tickets and took their places in the auditorium just as the quartet were arriving on-stage. There followed a program of English chamber music, each item being preceded by a short introduction from the leader, Martin Claver, giving biographical information about the composers, in such a way as to introduce the mainly Finnish audience to English music. It struck George Mason, as he listened, that Finns would be far more familiar with German music, besides having a fair number of native composers in addition to Sibelius. Each introduction was followed by a poem by a well-known author, such as Auden, John Betjeman and Ted Hughes. Applause at the conclusion was appreciatively polite, if not over-enthusiastic, and the visiting ensemble seemed pleased enough with their reception.

Mason managed to catch a word with Claver afterwards, as the public began filing out and the musicians were packing their instruments.

"That went very well," he said. "I particularly enjoyed the Gustav Holst and the Benjamin Britten."

"On vacation?" the lead violinist enquired, gratified at the compliment.

"A business trip, in a manner of speaking," the detective replied, without elaborating. "This is my assistant, Alison Aubrey."

"How do you do, Ms. Aubrey?"

"Very well, thank you," she replied. "It was a fine performance. I think the audience really appreciated it."

Martin Claver was more circumspect.

"It's a hard sell, promoting English music in Finland," he said. "They have so much home-grown talent. Klami, Rautavaara, Salinen, to name just a few."

"Are you on a European tour?" George Mason then asked.

"Not exactly," came the rather diffident reply. "We fulfill engagements here and there, when invited. Last week we were in Stockholm, for example. After tomorrow, our last day in Helsinki, we move north to Vaasa, on the west coast."

"Ever played in Holland?"

"We were in Amsterdam in March. Round about Queen Day. The city was covered in orange bunting."

"Was your reader with you?" Mason asked. "The person who recited the poems just now?"

"Jacob Phipps?" Claver said. "Yes, he was, as a matter of fact. He's with the National Theater, but he will not be going up to Vaasa with us. A new play in which he has a leading role opens in London later this week."

"We wish you every success in your future engagements," the detective said, on parting.

"If you happen to be in Vaasa on business," the other said, "I could get you complimentary tickets."

"That's hardly likely," Mason replied. "It's well out of our way. But thanks anyway. Perhaps in London, one day?"

Back outside, they made their way to Hotel Kivi to telephone Chief Inspector Harrington. By mid-afternoon, it seemed surprisingly warm for this latitude. The two detectives felt over-dressed compared with the denizens of Helsinki, who went about in shirt sleeves, and were glad to regain the air-conditioned interior of the hotel. They got through to Scotland Yard with minimum delay, spoke briefly with Harrington, and repaired to the bar for a cooling drink.

"What do you make of all that, George?" Alison asked, as she sipped chilled fruit juice.

"Jacob Phipps could fit the bill," her colleague replied.

"Because his first name begins Ja___?" she countered.

"Not only that. He is based in London and visited Amsterdam towards the end of March. He was, according to Martin Claver, recently in Stockholm and is now in Helsinki. As an actor and poetry reader, he would also be conversant with modern literature. That could explain the bizarre quotations left at the crime scenes."

Disinclined to waste a good thirst on soft drinks, he took a generous quaff of Paulaner, an imported German lager.

"We might be hard put to pin a motive on him," Alison observed.

"Harrington will look into that for us. Phipps may well have interests in property. Most people have and, along with others, he may have suffered significant losses in the market downturn. Everything else seems to fit quite well."

"Have you given up on Walter Cornelius?"

George Mason shook his head adamantly, took another swig of ale and said:

"Nobody has any idea where that person is, unfortunately. He's completely gone to ground. Captain Ivor Wells recently informed me by e-mail that his house in Meredith has now been sold."

"There was no sale sign visible when we were there," Alison remarked.

"The contract went through privately, through an estate agent in Meredith. It was already on track while we were there, but we were not aware of the fact. Nor, apparently, was Ivor Wells."

"Quite an elusive entity, this Walter Cornelius."

"You can say that again."

Just then, the receptionist called them to the telephone for the return call from London. Leaving their drinks momentarily, they crossed to the foyer.

"Pro Thespis did perform in London in March," Bill Harrington informed them. "They did Albee's Who's Afraid of Virginia Woolf? My sister-in-law and a friend went to see it, as a matter of fact. Thoroughly enjoyed it, too."

"Do you have relevant dates?" Mason asked.

"The play ran at the Shaftesbury Theatre during the week ending March 18."

"That could well be significant," Mason remarked. "Anything on Jacob Phipps?"

"Donald Dinwiddie is looking into the property angle. I don't expect he'll have much for you for a day or two. Make good use of your time and go easy on expenses."

"This evening, we're off to The Dolphin, Helsinki's most exclusive restaurant, down on the waterfront," Mason announced. To forestall his chief's likely apoplexy, he added, "Major Forsenius is treating us."

"He darned well better be," a blustery Bill Harrington exclaimed, "or you'll be up for misuse of public funds."

"He sounds happy," Alison Aubrey jocularly remarked, as they returned to the bar to finish their drinks before returning to meet Forsenius back at Police Headquarters.

"He'll give me rocket when we get back home, for winding him up," Mason explained. "Bill Harrington and I go back a long way and have grown quite used to each other's quirks and foibles. Beneath his gruff exterior, there beats a heart of gold."

"That's reassuring to hear," his companion said, in a not very convinced tone.

As they left the foyer, they hardly noticed an individual who was standing by the magazine rack, ostensibly scanning the pages of Newsweek, which the hotel stocked for the benefit of its English-speaking guests. The individual in question waited until the oddly-matched couple had re-entered the bar before approaching Reception.

"Rather unusual, isn't it," he enquired of the duty clerk, "to have English visitors so early in the season?"

"A little," the clerk replied. "But we do sometimes also see them in the early spring. Outdoor types, mainly, on their way to the fells of Lapland to ski."

Jason Milne, who had recently registered at the hotel, slid a ten-markka banknote across the desk.

"Business types, are they?" he enquired, disingenuously.

The clerk, quickly pocketing the banknote, leaned forward and said in hushed, almost conspiratorial tones:

"A short while ago, I placed a call for them to – would you believe it? – Scotland Yard! We certainly don't get many Sherlock Holmes types staying at Hotel Kivi."

The actor took a step backwards, in genuine astonishment.

"You can't be serious!" he exclaimed.

"It's the truth. Beyond that, I can tell you nothing. Client confidentiality, you understand?"

"Could be that a British V.I.P. is due to arrive, and they are part of an advance security team."

"That is certainly a possibility," the clerk agreed. "There's a follow-up meeting to the Helsinki Accords, scheduled for Monday. The French Embassy has booked dinner here for its staff on Sunday evening. They're even flying in a top chef from Paris."

Jason Milne repaired to the hotel bar, occupied a table on the far side of the room and observed the English couple with greater interest. Nursing his glass of Bourbon, he mused on the possible reasons for their presence. They could be, as the hotel clerk suggested, members of a security team arrived in advance of the high-level conference. Or they could be in the Finnish capital in connection with the incident at Karelia Pankki. That could imply that the police had linked the incident at National Indemnity, in the City of London, with the attempt on the life of Urpo Koivonen, and perhaps also with events in Amsterdam and Stockholm. He could only conclude that Milovan Piric had left clues behind him that investigators had picked up. So much for the Serb's professionalism, he ruefully reflected. Within fifteen minutes, the English pair had downed their drinks and were heading out of the bar into the broad afternoon sunlight.

It occurred to him to follow them at a discreet distance, to see whom they met. But he quickly reassured himself that the series of bank hits were all done by proxy, and that the hit-man was now dead. The police could have no knowledge of the existence of a Jason Milne, unless they were familiar with old movies, let alone of his involvement. Smiling inwardly, he slowly sipped his whiskey and congratulated himself that he would soon be on his way to Tallinn, where he was to perform one of his favorite roles. He would also be leaving the crime scenes well behind him.

*

Viljo Forsenius had just returned from Lahti by the time the Scotland Yard pair, more lightly dressed on account of the afternoon heat, arrived at South Harbor. As they entered his office, he switched on a large ceiling fan to circulate the air.

"Enjoy the performance?" he enquired.

"Very satisfying," George Mason said, "to hear English music performed here, even if it's a bit like taking coals to Newcastle."

The Finn chuckled.

"You mean we have so much native talent that we don't need to import more? In fact, we as a nation have become quite anglophile since the war. Practically everyone is learning English; whereas previously German language and culture were the dominant foreign influences. We even thought at one stage of offering the Finnish crown to a German prince."

"But you became a republic instead," Alison Aubrey remarked, "on gaining your independence from Russia?"

"That is correct," the gratified Finn replied. "We often feel such a small, marginal country, outside the mainstream of world affairs, that we wonder foreigners know much about us at all. I am pleased to note that you are both exceptions to the rule."

"We do our best to keep well-briefed," George Mason replied.

"Did the event help with your investigation?" Forsenius then enquired.

"It furnished a possible lead," Alison Aubrey replied. "And we did call by the Swedish Theater, on your suggestion, to obtain last week's program. It gives the complete itinerary of the Pro Thespis tour. Unfortunately, it does not list the cast."

"That's probably to allow for last-minute replacements," the Finn surmised. "Or changes necessitated by sudden absence or indisposition. On an extended tour such as this, any number of things could happen to troupe members, so they will have several actors in reserve and probably rotate them."

"We really do need names," George Mason urged.

Forsenius turned to his computer.

"Their web-site should provide an up-to-date list of company members," he said, keying in Pro Thespis. "But that does not necessarily mean they are all taking part in this tour."

The two visitors waited patiently for results and, a few minutes later, he handed each of them a print-out.

"It seems they're based in Portland, Maine," Mason remarked, casting his eye down the list of professional actors. "And there are, in fact, three whose forenames begin Ja___."

"James Barlow, Jason Milne and Janet Worsley," Alison read aloud. "Trouble is, according to this, they are about to move on to Tallinn, which is to be their final engagement."

"Death of a Salesman," George Mason said. "It's my favorite Miller play, about the shattering of the American dream. I've always had a lot of sympathy for the title character, Willie Loman, up against it in a competitive society and down on his luck."

"You may get to watch it again," Forsenius said, "in the event that you travel to Estonia."

"Wait a minute," Alison said. "This can't be the Jason Milne who has played in Hollywood movies...or can it?"

"You mean you have actually seen him perform?" an intrigued George Mason asked.

"Absolutely sure of it, if it is the same person. He played the lead in several films I've seen, going back a few years, mind you. Incident at Monte Carlo, for one."

"Could there perhaps be two actors named Jason Milne?" the major put in.

His not entirely rhetorical question caused a few moments' silence, before a pensive Mason said:

"I can think of a way we might find out."

"Which is...?"

"Who's Who in America? I don't imagine for one moment that you have a copy of it here at Police H.Q., but a good library might."

Viljo Forsenius at once picked up the phone and placed a call to Helsinki Central Library. Replacing the receiver after a short interval, he regretfully shook his head.

"They have the British Who's Who? but not its American equivalent, I'm afraid."

"Try the university," Alison suggested.

The Finn dialed again, and there ensued another flood of lilting, incomprehensible Finnish. This time, his face brightened.

"They have last year's edition," he proudly announced, "in the main reference section. But not the current one."

Mason and Aubrey exchanged glances.

"That should suit us quite adequately," Mason considered. "I imagine they alter relatively few entries each year in publications of that type. Add a few, delete a few. That sort of thing."

"Then you had better get down there, before they close for the day," said the Finn, anxious to complete his paperwork on the Lahti trip. "Report here first thing tomorrow morning and we'll take things from there."

"If we draw a blank," Mason said, "we still have Jacob Phipps to follow up on, pending Chief

Inspector Harrington's and our forensic accountant's findings."

"Is he still enjoying his malt whiskey?" the Finn wryly enquired.

"You bet," Alison Aubrey replied. "And he switches brands quite frequently."

Half an hour later, they were at Helsingin Yliopisto Library, leafing through Who's Who in America?, surrounded by young students doing research or using laptops.

"No mention here of a James Barlow, Alison," Mason remarked, checking the alphabetical entries."

"As a regular repertory actor, he's obviously not famous enough to be included," she observed. "Jason Milne may be a different kettle of fish, if he also appeared in Hollywood films."

Her colleague moved on to the M section. Eventually, staring him in the face, was the actor's name. He placed his index finger next to it and quickly drew his Alison's attention to the brief entry.

"Jason Milne," she excitedly read out, in hushed tones, so as not to disturb the nearby students. "Stage name of Walter Cornelius, born February 18, 1959 at Meredith, NH. Married Arlene Hilton, 1990. No children. Studied drama and performing arts at Concord University, MA, 1978-82. Appeared mainly in off-Broadway productions, prior to joining repertory company Pro Thespis, based in Portland ME. Film credits include Incident at Monte

Carlo and A Fatal Encounter. Nominated for best actor in…"

"No need to read it all," George Mason said, rising from his seat with a triumphant look and shutting the heavy volume with finality. "This looks like our man, all right, Detective Sergeant. We may well have cracked the case, thanks in no small part to your good self."

"Does that mean Paul Richardson is definitely off the hook?" a gratified Alison asked.

"I think we can safely rule him out, despite my earlier suspicions, based largely on coincidence. The evidence now seems to point in only one direction."

"I think this calls for a celebration," Alison Aubrey said, elated at having made another significant contribution to solving the case.

"We'll push the boat out tonight at The Dolphin, make no mistake," he replied. "It's the major's treat, but I shall insist on standing the wine."

"And a single malt with the coffee?"

"Cognac," her colleague rejoined. "We'll go one better than Bill Harrington."

*

Two days later, on the Thursday afternoon, the fine spring weather had taken a turn for the worse. George Mason and Alison Aubrey faced a rough crossing of the Gulf of Finland, against strong easterlies sweeping across the Baltic, on their way by Silja Line to Tallinn. Once there, they took a taxi to Police Headquarters, where Major Forsenius had arranged for them to meet with Captain Ari Seppala, a senior member of the local force. On the way, the visitors were struck by the well-preserved medieval aspect of Tallinn, especially the inner city, with its circular stone towers and pantiled roofs. The Major had briefed his Estonian counterpart in advance on the reason for their visit, and the Scotland Yard pair were anticipating a successful conclusion of the case.

"Welcome to Tallinn," Captain Seppala said, as they entered the modern suite of offices on the periphery of the inner city. "Major Forsenius tells me that you are reaching the end of a long investigation."

"Ideally," George Mason said, "we should like you to make the arrest, on Estonian soil, of the chief suspect in this case."

"You have sufficient grounds for this?" the Captain asked, offering them tea from a samovar. This was particularly welcome to Alison Aubrey, who was feeling a little queasy after the rough voyage.

"I understand that Major Forsenius has already given you some background?" Mason said.

"Only the merest details."

"There was an attempted murder in Helsinki last week of a bank manager named Urpo Koivonen," the Englishman explained. "The attack misfired, however, and it was the assailant rather than his intended victim who met his death."

"A pity that doesn't happen more often," Seppala, between sips of lemon-tea, sardonically observed.

"The Helsinki incident was the fourth in a series of assaults on bank managers, two of whom are now dead. The third, Willlem de Vries, of Zuider Bank, Amsterdam, has only recently emerged from a coma."

"And these incidents, according to your investigations, are all linked?" the Estonian asked.

"They all stem, to my way of thinking, from the deliberate over-valuation of a resort complex in the White Mountains of New Hampshire, followed by mortgage default leading to foreclosure. Our forensic accountant, Donald Dinwiddie, thinks this was a scheme purposely devised by the four bankers, or at least with their full knowledge. There is a similar case, currently before the High Court in London. The high valuation, ostensibly made by an independent firm, meant that the borrower got in over his head and would lose out in an economic downturn. He would be relying on people who bought units in the resort at inflated prices to keep up their loan re-payments in adverse circumstances."

"The bankers would then gain control of the said property at a knock-down price?" an amazed Ari Seppala asked, the light of understanding spreading across his alert features.

George Mason nodded.

"We at Scotland Yard," he added, "think that the borrower came to realize that he had been out-maneuvered. The slayings were his form of revenge."

"But he did not actually pull the trigger?"

"We are fairly certain that he hired a gunman to do the grunt work for him," Alison Aubrey said, sipping her welcome drink.

"And you consider that the instigator of these incidents is currently right here in Tallinn?" the Estonian asked, with a look of surprised concern.

"He is currently appearing in Arthur Miller's Death of a Salesman, at your National Folk Theater this week."

"Major Forsenius mentioned as much to me," the Captain said. "He also suggested that I book three tickets for tonight's performance."

The Scotland Yard pair exchanged looks of pleasant surprise.

"It's one of my favorite plays," George Mason said. "I should be delighted to attend an American production of it, by way of a change. I already saw Pro Thespis perform at Amsterdam, in a different Miller play. They're a first-rate company."

"And it will be a good opportunity," Alison Aubrey added, "for me to become acquainted with Arthur Miller."

"Be my guests," Seppala courteously allowed, before adding: "I am to arrest him directly after the performance? On what grounds?"

"On the grounds of complicity in the murders of Conrad Fields and Stig Lagerqvist."

"And after the arrest?"

"You detain him here in Tallinn until a formal extradition request is faxed from London, on charges in connection with the death of Conrad Fields, former manager of National Indemnity. It shouldn't take more than twenty-four hours."

"This is all a little irregular, Inspector, but I think we can bend the rules a little for you," the officer agreed. "In the meantime, my assistant will drive you to your hotel so that you can relax a little after what I gather was a fairly rough crossing. I will call for you at 7.15 p.m., for the short drive to the Folk Theater. There are several good restaurants in the vicinity of your hotel, if you wish to take advantage of them for an early dinner. I can recommend a glass of birch sap collected from the forests, in much the same way Americans gather maple syrup. It's a great restorative, which we Estonians often drink after sauna."

Alison Aubrey sensed that the captain had her in mind for that particular tip. They took leave of him with slight misgivings. The theater arrangement seemed fine enough, but dinner menus in Estonian? Mason had uncomfortable visions of salted fish and curdled milk.

*

The two detectives arrived at the theater a few minutes before the curtain went up. Captain Seppala collected the tickets he had reserved and quickly located their seats in the grand circle. Alison Aubrey had spent the remainder of the afternoon resting in her hotel room, to recover from the voyage; while her senior colleague had taken the opportunity to explore the fascinating purlieus of the old city, thinking he might not get another such opportunity. By early evening, Alison was more like her old self again and, having changed for the theater, joined her senior colleague for an early dinner at a restaurant noted for national dishes. With the cabbage soup and a main course of roast pork, they took the Estonian's tip and ordered glasses of birch sap, finding it rather sweet to the taste, but quite palatable.

As the curtain went up, they settled back in armchair seats to watch Death of a Salesman. George Mason was pleasantly surprised at the turn-out for an English-language play. The auditorium was three-quarters full, with professional types and younger people, probably university students, much in evidence. He found himself wondering just how much of the dialogue they took in, but his main focus of interest was the individual in the lead role, Jason Milne as Willy Loman, the salesman down on his luck.

Had the actor, Mason wondered, identified too closely with the title character? Had he sunk the proceeds of his acting career into the resort venture in the White Mountains and come badly unstuck? Certainly, he would not make that kind of money in repertory theater. And he was not getting any younger. Like Willy Loman, he may have felt that time and opportunity were running out. But he had reacted not in despair, but in anger, calculatedly arranging the deaths of those he had identified as his nemesis. Conflating the character with the actor, fiction with truth, as the drama unfolded, George Mason found himself beginning almost to sympathize with Jason Milne, until his professional instincts wrenched him out of his reverie. He was dealing here with a criminal mind with a theatrical touch, evidenced by the bizarre sequence of literary quotations.

"A fine actor, isn't he?" Alison remarked at the interval. "I enjoyed watching him in films, too, some years back."

"The language is a bit of a stretch for me," Ari Seppala confessed. "But I get the general drift."

"Quite an experience for you, I expect," Mason said, "having English – or American – theater here in Tallinn."

"We have had Shakespeare before now," the other replied. "And John Osborne's Look Back in Anger, as well as Joe Orton's Loot. My wife Silvi encouraged me to come. She teaches English at the high school and has complete fluency in the language. She would have joined us this evening, were it not for a parents meeting."

"I imagine they will have an understudy for Milne," Mason sympathetically remarked. "It would be a pity if they had to close the play early."

"They're sure to have one," Alison said, "in a touring company of this size. They have to allow for contingencies, such as sickness or family problems, as you surmised earlier."

The play resumed and the police trio followed it with rapt attention until its tragic conclusion. When the cast took their bows to enthusiastic applause, the officers left their seats in the circle, descended the stairway and made their way back-stage, meeting up with the lead actor as he was about to step into his dressing-room.

Jason Milne turned to confront them, a look of astonishment dawning across his taut features.

"You!" he exclaimed, recognizing George Mason at once, from Hotel Kivi.

The detective reacted in some surprise.

"Have we met before?" he tentatively asked.

The actor, without replying, turned to enter his dressing-room.

"Wait one moment," Ari Seppala then said, producing ID from his civilian clothes. "Jason Milne, I am arresting you on suspicion of complicity in the murders of Conrad Fields and Stig Lagerqvist."

"I haven't the faintest idea what you are referring to," the other archly replied.

"Does the name Milovan Piric mean something to you?" Mason asked.

"I know no one of that name," the actor adamantly replied, even as his face clouded.

"Yet you booked hotel rooms for him in Marienhamn and Stockholm, using a credit card in your real name, Walter Cornelius. This is your final curtain, Jason Milne, I regret to say."

The actor returned a curious sort of half-smile, conveying both shock and disbelief.

"You overplayed your hand," Mason then said, "with the quotations left at each bank. We figured they could not have originated with the likes of Milovan Piric, your hired assassin. There had to be a second party involved, someone with a wide knowledge of literature. That person, we eventually figured out, was you."

"Very impressive," the actor finally conceded, aware that the game was now up. "And did you identify the source of the quotations?"

"All except the third one," Alison Aubrey chipped in. "The one left at Vardagsbank, Stockholm."

"Business is other people's money?" Jason Milne, aka Walter Cornelius, said. "That is certainly true. Some parties will use other people's money without any qualms at all, purely for their own gain, if you let them. It's far simpler to do that than risk one's own money. Most of the finance industry is built on that premise, not to mention the ubiquitous conmen. Look at the subprime mortgage fiasco, to take just one instance."

George Mason thought at that point that the actor was going to elaborate on his motives, but he merely added:

"That particular quote is from Alexander Dumas, author of The Count of Monte Cristo. As a young actor starting out, I had a minor role in the original film version."

"I have seen some of your movies," Alison Aubrey remarked, with a show of feminine sympathy, "and I always enjoyed them."

"That's all water under the bridge now," the actor said, resignedly. "But I value your opinion nonetheless."

"We shall wait for you outside the theater," Ari Seppala then told him, "to give you time to change. Back at Police Headquarters, you will be given the opportunity to contact your lawyer, ahead of extradition proceedings to the United Kingdom."

"I noticed the pair of you at Hotel Kivi," Milne then said to Mason, "if you are curious as to how I recognized you. I marked you for a detective then, but I never imagined you would follow me here. I figured you were in Helsinki as security personnel, in advance of the coming conference."

"You mean we were all staying at the same hotel?" an astonished Alison Aubrey said. "How unlikely is that!"

Jason Milne nodded and returned a wry half-smile, feeling himself warm momentarily to the attractive young officer who had enjoyed his film roles.

"You are listed in Who's Who in America?" George Mason said, finally. "Your very celebrity, in a way, was your undoing."

The actor merely shrugged and stepped towards his dressing-table to wipe off his make-up, closing the door behind him.

CPSIA information can be obtained
at www.ICGtesting.com
Printed in the USA
BVHW030201300119
539033BV00001B/16/P

9 781492 830603